"*Nobody's Angel*
perfect. I won't t
writing classes a.
well to read Clark's story, which doesn't contain a wasted
word or a false note." ---The Washington Post

"The anecdotal structure pulls you along at just the right
pace and the economics of his story telling are
commendable. There's a world of intriguing and
memorable detail expertly packed into two-hundred
pages and just the right amount of heartache. The book's
close features one of the best final lines of any book I've
ever read. Please don't pick it up and read that last page
first, it's so worth getting there naturally."
--Barnes & Noble Ransom Notes:

"Heartbreaking... Captivating... Clark's true subject [is]
his city. Each page turn feels like real, authentic
Chicago." -- Chicago Sun-Times

"One of the best books of the year." --Bookreporter.com

Westerfield's Chain
"A pure delight for many reasons, not the least of which
is the way Jack Clark celebrates and rings a few changes
on the familiar private-eye script... There's a memorable
moment [on] virtually every page." --Chicago Tribune

"Jack Clark's descriptions are beautifully haunting and
his plotting is exceptional." --Romantic Times

"A likeable protagonist and spirited, uncluttered prose: a
promising debut by a Chicago cabbie who may drive a
hack but doesn't write like one." --Kirkus Reviews

BACK DOOR

TO L.A.

By Jack Clark

Back Door to L.A.

Published by Jack Clark Ink
        a desperation press

Copyright © 2016 by Jack Clark

www.jackclark.info
contactjack@jackclark.info

ISBN-13:
978-1479392544

ISBN-10:
1479392545

For

Hélène

&

To the memory of my brother
Vince Clark
1947 -- 2015

He was my first reader
from the beginning.

"Cut all that. This is where the story starts."

The show was breaking at Orchestra Hall. Half the audience was walking north up Michigan Avenue trying to flag southbound cabs. I sped past all those outstretched arms, around the cabs that had stopped for the lucky ones, and pulled to the doorman who was waving his arm and blowing his whistle. Behind him the patient and the infirm waited, most of them dressed to the nines.

The doorman opened my back door for the couple at the head of the line. "Thanks, Flash," he said, leaning into the cab, and then gave me an address on East Lake Shore Drive.

The woman slid in first. Her coat was open revealing a silver lining and a long black dress. Streaked grey-blond hair peeked out from under a colorful scarf. "Thank you so much," she said. Outside her husband handed the doorman a buck.

"Everybody's gotta make a living," I said. This was straight from Ace's rule book. *Always help out the doorman. He's working too.*

It was a warm night in February, which meant it was slightly above freezing, but the husband was dressed for the coldest night of the year: a long tan coat with fur around the collar and one of those Russian-style hats with furry flaps. He looked much older than his wife and he moved slowly and carefully with the help of a dark, carved cane. It took him a while to get into the back seat. Before the door closed behind him the doorman's whistle was howling again. I flipped on the meter and started away.

The guy leaned forward and stuck his head into the opening in the bulletproof shield. "One senior," he said, just as I was reaching to add the extra passenger charge.

"Okay," I said, and pulled my finger back.

"I fail to understand why cabdrivers do not know when the symphony ends," he said, and dropped back to his seat.

I went down a few blocks, got turned around and started back, past scores of people waving for northbound cabs. "I take it you don't have an answer," he said after I stopped for the light at Washington.

"Sorry. What was the question again?"

"Why are there no cabs waiting when the symphony ends?"

"You don't sit in lines on Saturday nights," I said.

"That makes no sense," he said.

"Why sit in a line when there's business everywhere?"

"Dear Mr. Cabdriver," he said, and he was back at the opening. "I put myself through college driving a Yellow Cab and I waited in plenty of lines on Saturday nights."

"I'm betting business was a bit different way back when," I said.

"Way back nothing," he said. "How long have you been driving?"

"Thirty years," I said. This was a bit of an overstatement.

"Which means you started about '83," he said. "And I quit on my 24th birthday which was in 1975. So, my not-so-young friend, it looks like we only missed each other by eight years."

"Congratulations on getting out," I said, and then I did a little math. "Wait a minute. You're not a senior." I reached out and rang up a dollar for the extra passenger charge. "And don't try to tell me your wife is."

"I'm sixty-two," he said.

"You get to take your Social Security early. Not your cab discount."

"He caught you, dear," his wife said. I glanced in the mirror and the two of us shared a quick laugh.

"Very funny," the man said. "You're both, very, very, funny."

"What's really funny," I said, "is you live on East Lake Shore and you're trying to beat a cabdriver out of a buck."

Their building was one of the ritziest in town, twenty-five or thirty stories of million dollar condos. But that wasn't high enough for some people. An heir to the Rockefeller fortune had built an entire house on top of the place a decade or two back.

One of the other wonders of the building was the turntable in the driveway. You pulled straight in, dropped your passengers, and then the doorman hit

9

a switch and turned you around. It was like a ride at Riverview back in the old days, without the speed or the cotton candy.

The doorman stepped out the moment we pulled in. "Nine-eighty-five," I said as the door opened behind me.

The guy handed me eleven dollars. "Hold on," he said, and a moment later dropped a quarter into my hand.

The woman walked to my window as the doorman helped her husband out the other side. "You made my day," she said, and slipped me a folded ten.

Her husband was next to stop by. "You're a very unpleasant fellow. Do you know that?" He limped away and followed his wife inside.

"And you're a cheapskate," I said, not loud enough for anyone to hear.

The doorman turned me around. I took a slow ride around the block and pulled into the Drake Hotel line behind three other losers.

"You know you're getting old when you find yourself sitting in hotel lines." This was my old pal Ace talking a few months before he finally retired.

Yet there I sat as the line crept slowly forward. It went against everything I'd learned. Suckers sat in lines. Hustlers got out and worked the streets. It was our biggest advantage over businesses with fixed addresses. We didn't have to wait for customers to walk in the door.

What was I thinking? Nothing. Time passed. The Sun-Times was on the seat beside me but it went unread. Sometimes I'd turn the pages, glance at the pictures and the headlines, but five minutes later I wouldn't remember any of it.

"You're a very unpleasant fellow." *Why was I letting that bother me?*

If nothing else, I knew I should get out of the cab. This was another of Ace's many rules*: Use any excuse to get your ass off the seat.* Check the back for trash, loose change, greenbacks, cell phones, and other lost objects. Wash the windows or just step out and stretch at a red light.

The doorman's whistle finally came. This time for a couple going to a Randolph Street high rise. Not a word was spoken until we arrived. "Keep it," the guy said, handing me a ten.

I headed towards the Loop, turned under the el at Wabash, and then pulled behind the lone cab sitting in the stand at the Palmer House. At least here, there was little danger of falling asleep. Every few minutes an el would rumble overhead and sparks would fall. For years, I'd been waiting to see a spark actually touch ground.

A few minutes later, one finally did. I was heading south--still under the el--when a Dispatch cab went shooting by at racetrack speed. "Jesus," my passenger said, as the cab passed with a blaring horn.

I caught his eye in the mirror. "Probably just off the boat." When I looked back at the road, the cab was in my lane, brake lights burning. I hit the brakes and the horn in the same instant and came to a screeching halt about a half inch from the cab's bumper.

The driver's door of the cab flew open and Ken

Willis trotted back my way. "Kenny, are you nuts?" I shouted.

"Eddie, call Ace at home. It's important."

"I got a load." I gestured towards my back seat.

"Yeah, me too," Willis said. "And he's not too happy right now."

I looked up. Ken's passenger was turned around looking our way. His arms were open. His hands out. I could almost read his lips: *What the fuck?*

"What are you doing in that?" I pointed at his Dispatch cab. He'd been driving an American-United for years.

"I could ask you the same question," he said. I'd recently switched to Flash. "Look, your daughter showed up at Greyhound. We've been trying to find you all night. Why don't you answer your phone?"

"My daughter?" I opened the door and stepped out to the street. "Laura?" I said, standing with the door open as taxis sped by just inches away. I hadn't seen her in nine years. *My little girl?* "She's here?"

"She's at Ace's," Willis said. "Call him."

"At Ace's? What's she doing there?" *Laura?*

"She's waiting for you, Eddie," he said. "Call Ace. I gotta run."

"Look, call him for me, okay?" I said. My phone had run out of juice days before. "Tell him I'm on the way."

"I can take another cab," my passenger said.

"No. It's right on the way. But thanks."

I felt like a real cabdriver again as I made every light down Wabash. "Can I drop you at the side entrance?"

"Perfect," the guy said as I turned left. "How old's

your daughter?"

I had to think for a moment. "Eighteen. Yeah. Eighteen. Her birthday was last month. That must be it. She's finally free." I flicked the meter off as we pulled alongside the Hilton. "On the house," I said. "Sorry about the stop."

"Here. Take this." He handed me a folded bill. "Buy your daughter a birthday present."

"Thanks," I said, then headed straight out to Lake Shore Drive and north.

The cab had wings. In seconds I was eight miles north sitting at the light at the end of the drive at Hollywood. I looked down at the bill still in my hand. Ulysses S. Grant smiled back.

TWO

I followed Hollywood into Ridge, both high-speed streets, and drove under a viaduct and past a convenience store closed for the night. I rarely passed this way without thinking of my old pal Lenny. He'd been killed by somebody he picked up right along here. The same punk had flagged me later that same week.

Tonight all I could think about was Laura Amber Miles, my little lamb. She was a little girl when I'd lost one job, then another. I became a drunk and before long I was divorced, an even bigger drunk, and a deadbeat father to boot.

I got so far behind in alimony and child support that my ex-wife hauled me into court. Her lawyer made me an offer. My ex would forgive what I owed--and she'd also drop a domestic battery charge--if I'd forget about Laura. And I had. I'd never even said goodbye. I'd signed papers agreeing not to see her until she'd turned 21. Before the year was out, my ex moved to California.

I'd talked to Laura once in all those years, on the phone and only for seconds. But that was enough to know she hadn't forgotten. *"Oh, Daddy, where have you been?"* she'd said before my ex had jerked the phone away. I'd had no defense. I'd done the unforgivable. I'd forsaken my only child.

Now she'd come home. I'd been dreaming about this day for years. But as I got closer and closer, I realized I was afraid. Hell, I was flat-out terrified.

Ace lived in West Rogers Park, on a quiet street of small post-war bungalows. Years ago the neighborhood had been predominately Jewish and many of Ace's neighbors had been fellow cabdrivers. They still were. But today most of them were Indian or Pakistani.

Doctors had told Ace to retire a few years back. He'd sold his taxi medallion for four times what he'd paid for it. But now that looked like peanuts, with medallions going for more than $300,000. He'd planned to sell the house too, and buy a travel camper and tour the country with his wife of fifty years. But before the house was sold, his wife had gotten sick and died.

Some of my fellow drivers joked that she just wasn't into roughing it.

Ace had taken the house off the market. He'd just put it back on. His new plan was a small condo in a high-rise overlooking the lake. "I spent enough time looking at traffic," he'd told me late one night. "All I want to see now are waves."

14

"Why not get a little sunshine while you're at it?"

"Too late," he'd said. "I'm an old man. All I know is this stupid town."

I parked but I had a hard time getting out of the cab. I found my cell phone charger and hooked that up, then wiped dust from the dashboard with a couple of fast-food napkins.

I walked down the block, up the steps, and then the fear really hit. The last time I'd seen her she'd been a little girl. Eighteen? She was almost a woman. What would I say to her?

"Relax. Relax," I told myself but I still couldn't ring the bell. I opened my wallet and pulled out the photo I'd carried for the last ten years. I'd put plenty of creases in it but they weren't enough to hide the love in a little girl's eyes. "I can't believe you're here," I whispered.

The door opened. "Eddie," Ace said. He stepped out to the porch and closed the door behind him. "She's out cold on the sofa." He was one of those guys who never seemed to age. He'd been a little old man when I'd first met him and he was still a little old man, though now with a little less hair.

"She's okay?" I asked.

"She's fine," he said. "She was exhausted. She wanted to stay awake until we found you."

"How did she get here?"

"Greyhound from L.A. Two days straight through, and I guess she was afraid to sleep. It was the typical lowlife convention."

"But how'd she get here?" I pointed straight down.

"Remember Wesley at Sky Blue?"

I shook my head. "What about him?"

"He was dropping someone at Greyhound and she walks up and asks if he knows you."

"Does he?"

"Well he'd heard about you, of course. And he drove her around until he found Paki Bob. Paki called Kenny. They tried to find you and, when they couldn't, Ken called me and I said bring her here. You're a lucky man, Eddie. You're getting a second chance."

Ace knew all about the deal I'd made with my ex. I'd actually bragged about it one night over coffee soon after we'd met. Ace didn't think I had anything to be proud of. "You'll regret that your entire life," he'd said. He'd gotten up from the table, left the restaurant, and barely talked to me for weeks.

"She's okay?" I said.

"Yeah. She's a good kid. Go in and see her." I followed him into a small foyer. The darkened living room was off to the left. I took a quick peek and a deep breath and decided I wasn't quite ready. I followed Ace down the hall to the kitchen.

A newspaper was open on the table with a coffee cup sitting alongside.

"Any coffee left?" I asked.

"Tea."

"Let me hit the head."

I went back into the hallway and took another quick look into the living room. What was I so afraid of?

I turned on the bathroom light and looked in the mirror, straight into a horror show. I was overweight. My hair was disheveled. I needed a shave. There were marks on my shirt from dribbled coffee and who knows what. A button was missing. My pants hung down.

Why hadn't I stopped home to change?

There was a single toothbrush in the rack. I pulled it out then changed my mind and did the best I could with a bit of toothpaste on a finger. I washed my face and ran fingers through my hair.

The living room curtains were drawn but they were thin enough that I could see the headlights passing on Western Avenue, a half block east.

The sofa's back was to the window. Laura was on her side facing the same way. Her blanket had come down a bit, exposing a small hand tucked beneath the shoulder strap of a thin shirt. The sound of her breathing took my breath away. I sat on the coffee table, put my hand over hers, and pulled the cover back up. "My little lamb," I whispered.

I don't know how long I sat there, feeling the warmth of her hand, listening to that steady breathing. "Daddy?" she said softly and tried to lift her head.

I could see it was a struggle. "Shhh. Shhh." I patted her head. "It's okay, Laura. It's me. Everything's okay."

"Oh, Daddy," she said and the head went back to the pillow and her hand gripped mine.

"Sleep, baby. Sleep."

"Love you," she said.

"I love you, too. Now go back to sleep. I'll be right here."

A few minutes later she began to toss and turn. "No, no, no," she muttered. Her head came up but her eyes stayed closed. "Don't let them take me," she whispered.

"It's okay, Laura. It's just a dream." I cradled her head in my hands and she dropped back to the sofa. "Nobody's taking you anywhere. Don't you worry about that."

THREE

Ace looked up from his newspaper. "Still sleeping?"

"Out like a light," I said.

"Ready for some tea?"

"You know, I think I'm gonna go home and change. Maybe take a shower."

"Eddie, you should be here when she wakes up."

I shook my head. "I don't want her to see me like this. I mean, look at me."

"I've seen you worse," he said. "Why not take a shower here?"

"Let me go home and get the place straightened out a bit. Christ, the windows haven't been opened in months. The bed isn't made. There's dirty dishes..." And suddenly I remembered what my apartment really looked like. "Oh, Jesus." There would be no fast way to straighten out that mess.

"Eddie," Ace said as he poured me tea. "You're her father. She doesn't care what your apartment looks like or what you look like. She loves you. She thinks you're a hero."

"Where would she get that?"

"Oh, me and Kenny, we built you up a bit. Your big night."

"My big night, where I almost got myself killed," I said. "Hey, can she stay here for a couple of days? I mean you got plenty of room. Or am I asking too much? I'll pay whatever you say."

"You'll pay? What kind of asshole are you? She can stay as long as she wants. Hell, I'd love to have her. It's been a long time." He stopped suddenly. I knew he was thinking about his wife. A moment later he shook his head and gave me a sad smile. "Upstairs is a mess. I'll put her in the den. That way she gets her own bathroom. We'll clear it out tomorrow. I've been using it as a sort of storeroom."

I realized my entire apartment was a storeroom. A storeroom for garbage. "I gotta find a new place to live," I said. "I mean, besides being a dump, it's not big enough for two people."

"Give you a good deal on this place."

"What'd she bring with her? Do you know?"

"It's all in one backpack."

"She'll need clothes and everything," I said. "We'll need furniture. Dishes. A couple of beds."

"Eddie, my friend," Ace said. "It sounds like you're finally gonna spend some of that money you've been so busy squirreling away."

For years all my cab-driving pals had been razzing me about all the money they thought I'd been saving. I'd always denied having any. But now I just smiled. "This is what it's for, Ace. This is what it's for."

"Come on," he said. I followed him to the den at the back of the house. "This used to be a porch." He flicked on the light. "Cost me a small fortune."

The room was a half moon with floor to ceiling windows. French doors led out to the backyard. There was a fireplace, a pull out couch, a couple of

19

easy chairs, a desk, and several bookshelves. A dozen cardboard boxes and several oversized plastic bags were scattered about.

"I've been clearing out upstairs," Ace said. "Nancy never threw anything away. It goes from here to the garage and then on to the Ark or Goodwill."

"She'll love it," I said, and then it hit me. "I don't know anything about her. I feel like I'm not even her father."

"Don't worry," Ace said. "She's a good kid."

"You know about as much as I do."

"I got a pretty good idea what kind of kid she is. We talked for hours. What do you think we were doing while we waited for you to turn up?"

"So why's she here? Why now? I'll bet she had a fight with her mother."

"Oh, sure," Ace said. "Like every teenage girl. And, big surprise, she doesn't like her stepfather, either."

"That leaves hope for me," I said.

"And, of course, they don't think too much of her boyfriend."

"Boyfriend?"

"She's eighteen, Eddie."

"So who is he?"

"Kid with good taste, you ask me."

The tea kettle whistled. Ace turned it off then filled a ceramic teapot.

"She's not pregnant?" Is this what I was so afraid of?

"Look, she's a good kid, Eddie. Trust me on this. She's smart. She's funny. But she's still a kid. We were idiots at that age. They've gotta be bigger idiots. I mean, look at the world."

And there she was standing in the doorway wiping sleep from her eyes. She was so beautiful I almost cried. I would have recognized her anywhere. The girl I'd given away.

"Hey, baby," I said, and engulfed her in a hug.

"Hi daddy. I'm so glad you came."

"You're glad I came? Oh, my god, baby. Oh, my god." I couldn't let her go. She smelled like a beautiful spring day. The first spring day in years.

After a while I took a few steps back, keeping my hands on her shoulders. "Let me get a look at you," I said.

Her hair was brown, cut short, and much lighter than I remembered. She was a bit on the thin side but she had a nice, healthy looking tan, and big brown eyes that sparkled like gold. She'd inherited her mother's nose, which was a major blessing.

Her T-shirt was so thin you could almost see through it and it wasn't very long. It stopped just above her belly button. The same belly button I used to blow on to make funny sounds. Her jeans were faded blue with plenty of holes and arty patches. They were a little on the tight side. The buckle was open and the zipper was halfway down, exposing striped underpants.

"Your barn door's open," I said.

"Huh?" Her eyes got wide when she smiled and tiny dimples appeared in her cheeks.

"Your zipper," I said, and I pointed.

"Oh." She took a deep breath and pulled the zipper up. "My barn door?"

"That's what we used to say," I said. "Your barn

21

door's open and the horses are getting out." I turned to Ace. "Wasn't that it?"

"You're flying low. That's what we said in the service."

Laura sat down and then pulled her feet up to the front of the chair. One of the ugliest spiders I'd ever seen was tattooed on her left ankle.

"Laura!" I couldn't stop myself. "That'll be with you your entire life."

"It's a stick-on," she said.

"It sure looks real."

She shook her head, and there were those dimples again. "Mom told me you have one."

"She did, did she?"

"This I'd like to see," Ace said.

I rolled up a sleeve to show my long-faded tattoo.

"What is it?" Laura asked. That's how bad it now looked.

"Baby, that was my very first car."

They couldn't stop laughing. "A car?" Ace said. "You got a tattoo of a car?"

"Hey, at least I got one," I said. "Where's yours?"

He took off his sweater and rolled up a sleeve to expose a bulldog primed to attack. "USMC," was written on the dog's helmet. "Chosin Reservoir, 1950."

"What's Chosin Reservoir?" Laura asked.

"It's a place I never want to see again," Ace said. "It's part of North Korea now."

"You were in Korea?" I asked.

"Was I in Korea? I froze my frigging butt off."

22

FOUR

"You're making me blush," Laura said.

"I just can't stop looking at you," I said. "I love your smile. I love your dimples. I love that you're here."

"They're not really dimples," she said, and her eyes went down.

"Don't tell me they're selling stick-on dimples now."

"They're for my studs," she said. "Mom took 'em out while I was sleeping and she wouldn't give 'em back even when I turned eighteen." She put a finger to one cheek and then the other. "I had a star here and a half moon here."

"You pierced your cheeks?"

"Now you sound like mom."

"Sorry, baby, just let me get used to this."

"And I'm not a baby anymore."

"Laura," Ace said. "You want some tea? You hungry?"

"I'm starving," she said. And there were those holes in her cheeks again. They weren't quite as cute as they'd been just a minute before.

"How about I scramble up some eggs," Ace said. "Bacon, potatoes, toast, what do you say?"

"If it's not too much work," I said. "You want help?"

"Why don't you guys sit down and get reacquainted," Ace said. He led us to the living room and turned on the lights. "I'll call when it's ready."

Laura sat cross-legged on the sofa with a folded blanket in her lap. I dropped into an easy chair.

"Laura," I said, and the words wouldn't come.

"This is so weird," she said. "We're like strangers."

"Look," I said after a while, "I'm your father. But I can't pretend that I'm the boss or anything. And yeah, I admit, I'm not a fan of tattoos even though I've got one myself. And I think it's pretty strange to start drilling holes in your face. But you're eighteen years old. And even if you weren't, I have no right to tell you how to act. Not after what I did to you."

"It's okay. You don't have to."

"Just let me say this. I know I did you wrong. I should never have let her take you away and I'll do anything I can to make it up to you."

"It's okay. It's okay. I kind of know what happened."

"You know what happened? This I'd like to hear."

"How you lost your job and couldn't find another and you and mom were fighting all the time and then you started drinking more than you should."

"That's pretty close," I said. "I thought your mother would make me out even worse than I was."

"Well, she did at first. She hated you. But then it happened again with Dan."

"What did?"

"He lost his job and he couldn't find another and mom and him were fighting and throwing things and he got into drugs really bad and they split up."

"They got divorced?"

"Separated. And we lost the house and me and

mom had to move into this tiny little apartment with no pool, no grass or trees or anything."

"So are they getting back together?"

"He says he wants to. But I'm not so sure."

"He find a job?"

"Yeah." She rolled her eyes. "As a drug dealer."

"Really?" *Why did this cheer me up?*

"Well he doesn't go to work. He drives a brand new beamer and he's always got money."

"That doesn't make him a drug dealer."

"And I found some once, before we lost the house. I went in to use the Jacuzzi and there was this big ball of aluminum foil all wrapped up. So I unwrapped it and it was all this white powder. It sure looked like drugs."

"So what'd you do?"

"I didn't do anything. He started pounding on the door for me to let him in. So I did. And he went right to the Jacuzzi and got the ball."

"Hmmmm. Well, I guess it's a good thing you're here, huh?"

"Yeah."

"So you plan on hanging around awhile?"

"Guess so."

"Good. So what do you want to do?"

"Well, I'd like to go to college sort of. But I still have to finish senior year."

"So we're going to have to find you a school. And we've got to find a place to live, 'cause I pretty much live in a shoebox. So that's the first step. Do you mind staying here until we can find a place big enough for both of us?"

She shrugged. "If that's what you want."

"I want you with me," I said. "But my place is so small and it's such a wreck, I'd be embarrassed to let you see it. How about you give me a couple of days to clean it up. Can you stay here that long? Don't worry. Ace is a good guy."

She nodded. "He's nice," she said. "It's just that blood is blood, right?"

"Of course," I said. But it would be weeks before I really understood the truth of those words.

"Hey, do you remember after you moved out, you used to pick me up from school, and we'd go on these really long drives? I remember one night you took me on this road that went right over the steel mills."

"The Skyway."

"And there were like these huge chimneys with giant flames shooting out right below us."

"Most of the mills are closed now," I said, and I remembered the reason for the drives. I didn't know what else to do with a little girl. Before I found the cab most of my friends were barflies. "Yeah, we used to drive and drive." Until she fell asleep in the car and the bars were safely closed.

"When my friends would ask me what Chicago was like, that's what I always told them, about that really high road and the steel mills in the night."

FIVE

Laura said she'd be fine sleeping on the living room sofa, but Ace wouldn't hear of it. We left her to finish her breakfast and Ace and I went back and did our best to straighten up the guest room. We stacked the boxes and bags in one corner, made a path to the bathroom and got the hide-a-bed open.

Ace went upstairs for towels and bedding. When he came down he said, "She's in there doing the dishes. It must run in the family."

"What's that?" Laura asked, standing in the doorway.

"Hard work," Ace said. "Your dad used to be the hardest working guy in town."

"I don't know if I'd go that far."

"You never wanted to quit," Ace said.

"I didn't have any money," I said. "That's how I lost you. Money. That's about all your mom and I ever fought about. Hell, we might still be together if it wasn't for that. We both loved you. So yeah, that was one of the great things about the cab. You could work all you wanted."

"And did he ever," Ace said.

"I'd drive all day. Go home, count my money, get a couple hours sleep, and then come out and drive all night. I used to love counting the money. That used to be my favorite part."

"We had to practically tie you to a chair at the roundtable so you'd have a second cup of coffee."

"What's the roundtable?" Laura asked.

"Coffee shop hangout," I said.

"Whole bunch of cabdrivers complaining all night long," Ace said.

"If I remember correctly," I said. "You were complainer-in-chief."

Ace pointed at Laura. "What'd you need, doll?"

"Do you have any kitchen cleanser?"

"Hmmm," Ace said. "Let me see about that." They went off to the kitchen.

Ace was back in a minute. "You drove the Polack nuts," he said.

"God, I miss him," I said. This was our old friend Polack Lenny, murdered for a couple hundred bucks.

"He couldn't stand you giving Yellow Cab all that money."

"Hey, what's Kenny doing at Dispatch?"

"Bernie sold out." Bernie was a private owner with several cabs. Ken had been driving for him for years. "Nobody can pass up the money," Ace said.

"It's like musical chairs," I said. The Russians and the New Yorkers had started buying Chicago taxi medallions by the bushel load and prices were going up accordingly. Small private owners and big fleets were selling out as fast as they could, leaving their drivers scrambling to find cabs.

"You know I never would have sold my medallion if I'd known Nancy was going to . . ."

"What you mean is, you never would have sold it if you knew prices were gonna go through the roof."

"Well, sure," Ace said. "That, too."

We finished making the bed, got the bathroom ready, then we sat down and talked some more about our favorite subject: the cab business.

"I got lucky tonight," I said as Laura walked in. "Guy gave me fifty on a trip from the Palmer House to the Hilton."

"Eddie, I've told you before. Never mess with another man's money."

"He knew what he was doing."

"No way. He thought he gave you a ten."

"No. No," I said. "He was in the cab when Kenny

told me about Laura. I must have said something about how it was just her birthday"--I gave her a wink--"so when he got out he gave me the fifty and said I should buy her a birthday present. Which is exactly what I'm gonna do first thing tomorrow."

"Okay. Maybe this time you're right. But what about all the other times?"

"If people are gonna be that careless with their money."

"Here," Ace said. "Let's let Laura be the judge. Here's the question. It's seven dollars on the meter and your passenger hands you a hundred dollar bill and says, `Give me a buck back.' What do you do?"

This brought a big smile to Laura's face. "That actually happens?"

"More often than you might think," I said. "But not usually with a hundred."

"I've had hundreds four or five times," Ace said.

"So what do you do?" Laura asked.

"I hold it up so they can see it," Ace said, "and I say, 'That's gonna be the best tip I get all week' or something like that."

"And what do you do, dad?"

"Well, maybe I'm not setting a good example here," I said--and I tried to savor the way the word dad had so easily slipped off her tongue--"but I give 'em what they asked for. I figure if they're that careless with their money, better me than the next guy."

"But it's their money," Ace said. "Not yours." He could get very passionate on this subject.

"Wait," I said. "Why don't you tell her what happens when somebody leaves a twenty on your back seat?"

"Well, here's where I agree with your dad," Ace said. "I keep it."

"So what's the difference?" I asked.

"Number one," Ace said. "I'm not even sure it's their money. Could be the guy before."

"Say it's your first load."

"Okay. Fair enough. So I know it's his. Well, it's like you say, if he's that careless with his money. But see, the difference is, I didn't have anything to do with it. I didn't mess with his money. He did."

"Laura, honey," I said. "What do think?"

"It's kind of confusing," she said, and she looked like she was having a hard time with Ace's fine distinction.

"Laura," Ace said. "Go get your little book."

She went out and came back with a small pink book with a metal zipper. It was about the size of a standard paperback.

"Now write this down in big letters," Ace said. "'Never mess with another man's money.' It's one of life's most important rules. And don't pay any attention to your father here. Being poor sort of messed up his morals."

Laura unzipped the book which was covered with stars and other stickers. She found a page and started to write. It took her a while. She kept starting and stopping. I thought she might be having trouble with the pen or maybe her spelling wasn't so good. But when she finished, she looked up and there were tears in her eyes.

"Laura, you okay?" I asked.

"I'm just so tired," she said.

"Well, I better get out of here and let you get some sleep," I said.

"I'm so sorry," she said. It looked like every ounce of energy was gone.

"Baby, you got nothing to be sorry about," I said. "Now get some sleep. I'll pick you up about noon and we'll go shopping. How's that sound?"

SIX

I had a hard time getting to sleep. I kept jerking awake, wondering if the entire night had been a dream. My little girl had finally come home. But I couldn't quite see her in my mind. I remembered the dimple-stud-holes and the big brown eyes but I couldn't put them into a face. In the morning light the whole idea seemed ridiculous. What would I do with a teenage girl?

I was out the door just before noon, and was soon in the back seat of a northbound taxi cruising up Western Avenue in a light rain. Past Foster Avenue the driver put both feet to the gas pedal. He must have been doing sixty, twice the limit. He was just a few inches off the parked cars.

Rosehill Cemetery was on the right. There were no cross streets for close to a mile. It was a natural place to speed. And years ago this had been a favorite stretch for the radar cops. But then the police department disbanded the Traffic Division. This was because many of the cops were filling their pockets, not their ticket books. Now the city had red light cameras and speed bumps instead.

We were two blocks south of Peterson Avenue when the right-side mirror exploded. The driver was the most surprised guy on the block. He actually slowed down a bit. "What was that?"

"Your mirror," I said. "You hit a mirror on a parked car. I think it might have been a Yellow Cab." I'd seen a flash of yellow as we'd sped past.

"I will drop you and then go back," he said with a Middle-Eastern accent.

"Sure you will," I said.

The light at Peterson turned red in front of us. The driver laid on the horn and blew right through. The red light camera flashed and snapped pictures. That was a ninety dollar fine.

"How long you been driving?" I asked.

"Six months."

"You know, I've been driving quite a bit longer than that. Could I give you some advice?"

"You are a driver yourself, sir? A taxi driver? You are going to pick up the cab?"

"I'm the night driver. I don't get it until six."

"I drive nights, day, all the time."

"Like counting that money, huh?"

"You are a driver for sure," he said. He turned and gave me a big smile.

"Here's all I wanted to say. If you're gonna drive that fast, move over to the left lane. It gives you more time to react if one of those cars suddenly decides to pull out. And then you don't have to worry about your mirror."

"But if I am in the right lane and someone turns left, I don't have to worry."

"And every so often a radar cop will be sitting back there. You're not gonna see 'em in time if you're in the right lane."

"I have never seen radar cops there. Farther south, yes. There, no."

"Never for you is six months," I said. "You know the camera got you."

"I know," he said. "Ninety dollars. It has happened before."

"Another reason to slow down," I said.

"I would have made the light if it wasn't for that Yellow Cab."

You couldn't argue with logic like that, I decided, and didn't say another word until Ace's block came into view.

SEVEN

"Your little girl's down in the dumps," Ace said and stepped out to the porch. "And something funny. I think she might have slept in the bathroom."

"The whole night?"

He shrugged. "Not sure. I wanted to say goodnight but it looked like she was gonna be in there forever so I finally gave up. Then this morning when I came down, she was in there again and the blankets and pillows were gone too."

"Strange," I said. "Maybe it's just too cold for her."

The door to the guest room was open but I knocked anyway. "Come in," she said, but I didn't see her at first. The bed was back to being a sofa.

I finally found her on the floor by the cold fireplace, almost lost inside a pile of oversized pillows. She was facing the yard where there wasn't a hint of green. Her California tan seemed to have faded overnight. She looked like the typical, pale, mid-winter Chicagoan.

"Hello, beautiful."

"Does the sun ever shine here?"

"You really want to see the sun, come when it's about ten below. There won't be a cloud in the sky."

"It doesn't get that cold."

"Colder," I said. "Hell, it was below zero when you were born, if I remember correctly."

"Maybe that's what happened to me," she said.

"What's wrong?"

"Nothing really."

"Come on. You can tell me."

"Oh, I'm just tired I guess. I didn't really sleep much and the long trip and everything."

"I heard you didn't sleep at all on the bus," I said.

"I closed my eyes one time and the next thing I knew someone was going through my bag. I screamed so loud I woke the whole bus."

"Good girl. So did they arrest him?"

"Arrest him? The driver never even slowed down."

"Ace has got tea made," I said. "What do you say? And then we'll go shopping. Or would you rather sit here and mope?"

"Let me think about that for a minute," she said, and that was the first smile of the day.

EIGHT

"I thought we'd start at Water Tower Place," I said on the way down Lake Shore Drive. I was behind the wheel of Ace's Toyota. It was ten years old but had only recently reached 50,000 miles.

"What's that?" Laura asked.

"Shopping mall in a high rise," I said. "Right

there," I pointed a few minutes later to a huge block of marble.

"It looks like a giant tombstone," she said.

Before long, we were walking down the aisles of Macy's. "These prices are ridiculous," Laura said. She held up a tiny sweater. "Three hundred and nine dollars. For this? My god, a foot of material and two buttons. No way."

We walked out to an interior atrium, and then went up and down the escalators and in and out of shops. Sales people did not rush to greet us. We didn't belong. We weren't tourists and we weren't rich. They knew it and we knew it, too. Laura kept checking the tags and then whispering the price to me.

"Don't worry," I said. "Believe me, if I can't afford it, I'll let you know."

"Eighty dollars for a T-shirt? Are they nuts? Who would buy this?"

"Lots of rich people in this town," I said.

"They must be stupid too," Laura said.

"You sound just like your mother," I said.

"She'd kill me if I spent eighty dollars on a T-shirt."

"Now what's this?" A sign said, *La Chambre Royale*.

"The Royal Bedroom," Laura translated.

"You know French?"

"Straight A's since freshman year."

"Hey, good work," I said. I led her inside where four beds were made up with colorful comforters, pillows and sheets. "We're both gonna need beds."

"Five thousand dollars," Laura whispered as I

flopped down on the first bed. I kept my feet on the floor as a saleswoman watched with a frown. "I think that's just the headboard."

"You gotta be kidding me." I popped back up and took a look at the sales tag. "Time to go," I said, and we went out the door. "Maybe if we just get a couple of pillows."

This sent Laura into a fit of giggles. "Five thousand dollars and you don't even get a bed," she said. "That's like the stupidest thing I ever heard."

"You know what's really funny," she said after we stopped for a snack at the food court, "Dan built me a brand new bedroom in his new house. Beds and desks and he had it all painted and everything. And he was telling me how generous he was because it cost all of two thousand dollars."

"Dan's your stepfather, right?"

"Yeah. He's a creep. He said the room was supposed to prepare me for college. So he like designed it to look like a dorm room."

"Well, that was nice of him," I said.

"No it wasn't," she said. Her eyes went down and she leaned away, as if she were afraid I might reach out and hit her.

"Laura, are you okay?"

Her eyes came back up but only for a second. "I just miss the old house."

"You sure you're okay?" I said.

She nodded and gave me a quick smile. "Hey, when you go shopping, where do you go?"

"There's a Sears right by my apartment," I said. "But you know years ago I picked up this lady right in front here, a tourist from France. It took me a while to figure out what she was saying. But it was exactly what you just said. And I said, 'What do you mean, where do I shop?' She said, 'I can't afford these prices. Take me to where you shop.' "

"You didn't take her to Sears?"

"No. Up around Belmont and Clark. There's a Marshall's and a big shoe store and all these little shops."

"Could we go there?"

NINE

Laura found a down jacket on sale at Marshall's. A sign said it would keep her warm to forty below. I had to promise that it would never get that cold. She got gloves to match and insulated boots downstairs at the shoe store. Before we left the building she had shirts and jeans, underwear, and running shoes. We locked everything in the car and then walked up to Belmont Avenue, where Laura fell in love with a black leather jacket. The zipper pull was the face of a snarling bulldog. It looked just like Ace's tattoo.

"We have to buy it," I said.

"I just got a jacket," she said.

"Ace is gonna love it."

"You think we can take the first one back?"

"You'll need that one when it gets really cold," I said.

It took me a while to talk her into it but I finally did. She wore the jacket out of the store. And then kept checking her reflection in the store windows as we walked along Belmont.

"Hey, nice leather," a girl dressed all in black said.

That added a bounce to Laura's step. "Can we

take the el somewhere," she asked, as a train pulled into the station overhead.

"Sure," I said, and we went up the stairs and got on a Loop-bound train.

Laura took the window seat and I pointed out the various sights. "You can see right into people's houses," she said.

In the seat in front a guy had the Sun-Times open wide.

"It was pretty cool seeing your picture in the newspaper," Laura said.

"Ace showed you that?"

"And mom had a copy."

"Your mother had a copy of the newspaper?"

She nodded. "I found it when I was looking for my birth certificate. I guess somebody sent it to her."

"That's funny," I said. *Why did this shock me so?* Not only did she have a copy; she'd filed it away with the important papers.

I'd made page five. CABBIE NABS KILLER. There was a small picture of me, a twin of the one on my chauffeur's license, and a not-very-accurate story about how I'd managed to catch Polack Lenny's murderer.

"That was the luckiest day of my life," I said. "Until you came back, that is."

"They called you a hero."

"You want to know what really happened. He dropped his gun and I picked it up. So if that makes me a hero."

"It's still pretty cool," Laura said.

"It beats the alternative. I'll tell you that."

The train squealed on the turns as it went around

the Loop, dropping off and picking up passengers at every stop. But this was a Sunday afternoon train and it was never crowded until we started the return trip north. At Fullerton, in the heart of Lincoln Park, a standing-room only crowd arrived.

"Looking good, girl. Looking good."

I looked up. He was 25 or 30, one of the straphangers filling the aisle. He had his own leather jacket and was looking down at Laura with the leer of a guy at a strip club. "Shut your mouth or I'll shut it for you," I said and I started to stand.

"Hey, I didn't mean anything." He held up his hands.

"Stop!" Laura said and pulled me back down. "What are you doing?"

"What's wrong?" I said when we were back on the sidewalk at Belmont Avenue.

"He was just trying to be nice."

"Come on, Laura. You're not that naive. And, no matter what, he shouldn't be hitting on you when you're with your father. Anyone knows better than that."

"He doesn't know you're my father. He didn't know we were together."

"I'm sitting right next to you."

"The train was full. And it's not like we look alike or anything."

That stopped me. "You don't think there's a bit of a family resemblance?"

"I was more thinking of how we're dressed. And, you know, I've got a sun tan and you're . . ."

Yeah. I was white as a ghost. And I remembered my reflection in Ace's bathroom mirror. "Maybe you're right," I said. "Sorry."

"Apology accepted," she said.

"Maybe I should get some new clothes, too."

"Yeah, like a whole new wardrobe."

TEN

We used Ace's car or the CTA during the day and the cab at night. We went shopping for clothes for both of us, for schools, for apartments, but when I look back it seems like one long drive. One where Laura was the tourist and I was the tour guide.

We drove by the old house in Avondale several times. It was just a block off the Kennedy Expressway, the route from O'Hare to the Loop. Laura remembered hearing the trucks and the trains at night. "I used to think there was this super ginormous train that just went on forever," she said.

"Ginormous?"

"That's like really, really, big."

I showed her the spot on Diversey Avenue where I'd worked as a project manager for an engineering firm.

"Do you ever think of doing that again?" she asked.

"I've been thinking about it a lot lately," I said. "I mean, do I really want to keep driving a cab? I'll never see you."

"Couldn't you just drive during the day?"

"I tried that once. It's a whole different business. Everybody's in a hurry. There's traffic everywhere. And everybody's mad `cause they're going to work. It's no fun at all."

"Mom says work isn't supposed to be fun."

"Hey, did you call her yet?"

She nodded. "I left a message."

"Good."

Laura got a kick out of the new city, the city of youth. She couldn't get enough of Lincoln Park, Wrigleyville, Wicker Park, and Logan Square. These were the streets where I spent too much of my working life, ferrying young punks and drunks around, people who looked just like that kid on the train. As a cabdriver these neighborhoods were impossible to avoid.

On my own, I was happier in the older parts of town, places without the loudness and the bright lights of youth, places where I could still feel the past, where a turn at some long forgotten corner might suddenly bring memories of old times. But as the years went on those old corners became harder and harder to find.

"Can we pick somebody up sometime?" Laura asked one night.

"Well, I'm not supposed to. But maybe. We'll see."

Ten minutes later, we were waiting at a red light in Lincoln Square when a slender guy in a light jacket waved.

"What do you think?" I said.

"Can we?"

I pulled towards the curb and popped the door locks. "Hey, buddy," I said as he climbed in.

"Devon," he said with a heavy south-of-the-border accent. He pointed straight ahead up Western Avenue.

"Just the corner up there?" I asked as I pulled away.

He didn't say anything, just pointed the same way. I looked back in the mirror. He was just a kid I saw, maybe a year or two older than Laura.

"You a cook?" I asked as we passed Foster Avenue.

"*No comprende,*" he said and he flashed a nervous smile.

'Bus boy?"

"*Si,*" he said, and the smile got wider. "Bus boy. Bus boy."

I dropped him on the corner of Devon and continued up Western towards Ace's. "That was so weird," Laura said.

"You never said a word," I said.

"I was afraid to," she said. "Isn't that funny?"

ELEVEN

The cemetery was in Hillside, one of the Western suburbs off the Eisenhower Expressway. We stopped for flowers in a place on Roosevelt Road then drove down the curving lanes looking for my parents' markers.

"What's in there?" Laura asked as we passed a mausoleum as big as an apartment building.

"Dead people," I said.

"You can be buried on the second floor? That's gross."

"Plastic flowers," she said, as we walked among the graves. "Who puts plastic flowers on a grave?"

"Quite a few people, apparently."

"Please don't put plastic flowers on my grave. Promise, okay?"

"I think it's gonna work the other way around," I

said. "But I'll save you the trouble, just cremate me, deal?"

"Where do I scatter the ashes?"

"Somewhere nice," I said. "The middle of nowhere. Nobody around."

"Sounds cool. Me too, okay?"

"By the time you die they'll have high-rise cemeteries. You can be buried on the 99th floor."

"Did you mean what you said the other day," Laura asked. "How you and mom could still be together?"

"That's probably wishful thinking," I said. "Some of it's hard to forget. She was a terror at the end."

"Yeah, because everything was on her shoulders," Laura said. "She told me she never felt so alone. You were gone. Well, you weren't really gone."

"No. You're right. I was gone."

"And she had to think about me."

"Yeah. I give her credit," I said. "I lost my job and she went right out and found one. But she didn't quit her part-time job. And did I help out? No. I was too busy feeling sorry for myself to even stay home and watch you. So she had to pay for a babysitter, too.

"She never lost the house. She paid so you could go to a good school. You always had enough to eat. Good clothes. She wouldn't let you wear hand-me-downs. And then she gets a nice promotion and they send her out to a conference in sunny California where she meets good-old Dan and just like that she's got a brand new family."

"You know how they met?"

"At the conference, wasn't it?"

43

"He pulled her over for speeding."

"He's a cop?"

"Yeah. Until he got laid off."

"How come I didn't know that?"

"That's why it's so scary."

"What?"

"I mean him being a drug dealer and all."

"I'm not following you."

"Well, most of his friends are cops. So he can do anything he wants and he'll always get away with it."

"Wait," I said. "Did you get in some kind of trouble with him?"

"Sort of."

"What?"

"Oh just, you know."

"Laura, come on, please. Tell me what happened."

"Nothing really," she said, but it didn't sound very convincing.

"Laura."

"He liked to just torture me sometimes."

"Torture you?"

"Just asking lots of questions. Interrogation, he used to call it."

"About what?"

"My friends," she said. "It's funny. I used to think he was looking for customers because he always wanted to know who was into drugs. But he wanted to know everything about them. Mostly my guy friends. It was like he was keeping a file. Were they straight or gay? What kind of car did they drive? What did their parents do? It just went on and on."

"Maybe he's gay himself," I said. Just the thought

cheered me up.

"No. I used to catch him looking at me sometimes."

"Like what?"

"Like, you know," she said.

"Like he's not your stepfather?"

"But it's not blood," she said. "He told me that once. That we weren't blood relatives and someday when I was older he might want to like hook up with me."

"Jesus Christ, Laura. Well, no wonder you left. Did you tell your mother?"

"That her husband's a creep? I don't think so."

We stopped at restaurants all over town. We'd sit across from each other but not much got said. Sometimes I'd catch her looking right at me and I'd think she was about to say something. But then she'd quickly look down.

For some reason that kid on the train kept coming to mind. "*Hey, girl, looking good,*" he'd said. And, just as I was telling him to shut up, I'd heard Laura say something, too. "*Thanks.*" Is that what it was? Or maybe it was just a return "*Hey.*" But she'd grown colder right there on the train and she'd barely warmed up since. Could a couple of words spoken in haste really have that big an effect?

As the days wore on, she talked less and less. I'd ramble on and on, asking about this, that, and the other thing, trying to keep the conversation going. But the more I talked the less she said. Why had she left California so quickly? I didn't know and she wouldn't tell me. "Oh, I just decided, you know."

I'd ask questions about her life and her sentences

petered off into nothingness. Or worse: "You're starting to sound like Mom." Or, worse yet: "You're starting to sound like Dan."

I spent more money in those few days then I'd spent in years. I wanted to spend more. But Laura didn't want a computer or a fancy phone. I told her I'd buy her a car when we got settled. But even that didn't seem to excite her.

"It's kind of neat you can live without one."

"Did you have a car in California?"

"Oh, sure," she said. "I had a really cool Toyota. Then Dan bought me a brand new Mustang and made me trade it in. And he bought Mom a Lexus and took her to Rio. He bought a big house in the valley and they were going to get back together and we were going to be one big happy family again."

"I take it, it didn't work."

"It was bullshit."

"What?"

"Everything," she said. "It was all bullshit."

TWELVE

I paid a maid service a hundred and fifty dollars to clean my apartment. When I went to pick up Laura, I found Ace waiting on the porch.

He stuttered and stammered for a bit. "Look, you gotta talk to Laura. She's been having nightmares. Last night she woke me from a dead sleep. I got down there and she's shivering and crying. She's been kind of hinting around about stuff. But I don't want to get between you two. You gotta talk. You're her father. But you gotta make it easy for her. She's just a kid."

"We're working on it. Okay?"

"Okay, Eddie" he said. "I just wanted to make sure."

I hadn't realized what a dump the Rosewood Arms was until I saw it through Laura's eyes. The lobby hadn't been cleaned in months. It was littered with takeout menus and junk mail. Several of the mailboxes had been pried open.

The elevator was one of those ancient cages with a thick outside door and a folding gate. I had to give the gate a kick to get it closed. The linoleum floor was faded and torn. It smelled like someone had taken a piss not long ago.

"This is kind of creepy," Laura whispered as we started up with a loud jolt.

Upstairs, various cooking smells wafted out as we walked down the long, narrow hallway. None of them were very appetizing.

My apartment looked pretty good, at least to my eyes. The kitchen and the bathroom sparkled like never before. The afternoon sun was shining in the windows. The wood floors shone brightly. The bedroom needed a new coat of paint but the comforter was cheerful, the dresser top was clean, and the mirror was crystal clear. The place even smelled nice.

"So what do you think?" I asked.

"It's nice," she said.

"So could you live here? You take the bedroom. I'll sleep on the couch."

"Sure. Okay." She stammered a bit. "That's fine." She parted a curtain and looked down to the alley with its overflowing dumpsters.

"Don't worry about hurting my feelings," I said. "Would you rather stay at Ace's until we find something?"

"That'd be okay, too," she said.

"Okay," I said. "That's settled. You stay at Ace's and we'll find a place we both like. Agreed?"

"It's not that I don't like it."

"Hell, I've been meaning to get out of here for years."

THIRTEEN

That night we passed by Division and Halsted, where the last high-rise in the Cabrini-Green housing project was being knocked to the ground. There'd been scores of buildings at one time. Now it was nothing but rubble.

"Where did all the people go?" Laura asked.

"Nobody cares," I said.

"But you care, don't you?"

"I care about the people. But I'm glad it's gone."

I didn't mention that my friend Polack Lenny had been murdered right around the corner. It turned out to have nothing to do with Cabrini.

"So what are they going to put here?" Laura asked.

"Fancy stores and people with money, more than likely."

"That's not fair."

"No," I said. "Hey, you really want to see where the people went?"

A cold drizzle was falling. It was the perfect night for a tour of the city's worst neighborhoods. The rain would keep most of the riff-raff off the streets.

We went west through trendy Wicker Park, south a half mile to Chicago Avenue, through the old Ukrainian neighborhood and, a mile later, blue-light police cameras were flashing on just about every corner, watching mostly empty streets.

On hot summer nights the whole neighborhood would be outside, kids in diapers and great-grandmothers who weren't yet fifty--the entire family--even at two in the morning. It was a dangerous place for a sightseeing cab driver, of course. But it was even more dangerous to not be passing through, to actually live here.

"Those are police cameras," I said. "Used to be drug dealers on every corner. They put the cameras up and guess what happened?"

"The drug dealers went away?"

"Yeah. But not too far." I drove two blocks to Augusta Boulevard and, even with the rain and another battery of police cameras, the drug dealers were busy working. They waved as we approached, trying to get us to buy from their corner.

"But they have cameras here too," Laura said.

"I don't know what to tell you."

A group of guys were hanging on one corner. Nobody waved but they all watched us approach. One guy stepped out and did a perfect imitation of someone flagging a taxi. I tooted the horn. "Dream on, buddy," I said, and he flashed a big smile.

"You wouldn't pick him up?"

"Not on a bet," I said.

"Just because he's black?"

"Laura, the good guys don't hang on corners

49

anymore. He didn't want a cab, anyway. He was just messing around. But if I stopped for him, I mean, come on. They're all going to think I'm a chump and even if they didn't start out planning to rob a cabdriver that might be how it ends."

"How about that guy?" she asked a block later, where a guy was hurrying from his car to a nearby house.

"Oh, sure," I said. "That's a working man. But he's not taking any cab. Even if he can afford to, he's not wasting his money."

"You think cabs are a waste of money?"

"They're a luxury," I said. "You can always get there cheaper."

We headed south past Madison Street and then Roosevelt Road, once thriving commercial streets. They'd been destroyed in the riots of the '60s and vast sections of both streets were still nothing but moonscape.

"How about that guy?" Laura asked, as we passed a guy waiting at a bus stop on Homan Avenue.

"Oh, yeah. Probably." And we continued south, playing our new game.

We went east on 26th Street, the heart of Little Village. "I've never had a single problem with a Mexican," I said. "Except they get so drunk sometimes they can't even tell you where they're going."

"They call that ethnic stereotyping."

"I call it way too much cervesa."

"What's that?" Laura asked as the bright lights of Little Village turned grey.

"Cook County Jail," I said. "Something like ten thousand inmates in there." And most of them came from the neighborhoods we were passing through.

We headed south and east. Before long police cameras were flashing again. But there was no longer much to watch. "This is Englewood," I said. "It's funny, ten, fifteen years ago this was the worst neighborhood in town. Kids were getting shot almost every day. So people got out, and the city condemned a bunch of abandoned buildings and others burned down. And now the police like to brag that the murder rate is down. Of course the murder rate is down," I said and Laura finished for me, "The people are gone."

In Englewood almost everyone walked in the streets. Many of the sidewalks were crumbled and if it snowed there was no one to shovel in front of all the empty lots. Half the street lights were burned or shot out. You could see for blocks through the emptiness.

"You asked where the people from the projects went. A lot of them ended up here, which just made it worse. And anybody who could get out did. And the rest are trapped."

"You know what's funny?" Laura said. "It almost looks like a frontier town in the history books. The streets all laid out waiting for the houses and the people to come."

For years Tony Golden, one of my cab-driving pals, had been talking about a vast City Hall conspiracy to get the poor out of Chicago. At the roundtable we usually laughed at his theory. But when I drove through Englewood or Lawndale or

East Garfield Park, not only did the conspiracy seem believable. It seemed reasonably successful.

We continued east into Hyde Park, took a quick look at President Obama's block with its police barricade, then headed for Lake Shore Drive.

"Did you ever pick up anybody famous?" Laura asked as we went north.

"Oh, sure."

"Like who?"

"Like John Malkovich, I picked him up one night."

"Did you talk to him?"

"No. He was with some other guy and they were talking. I picked up Ann Landers before she died."

"Who's that?"

"Advice columnist. You know, like Dear Abby."

"Did you talk to her?"

"No. I picked up this guy in a tuxedo and then we went and got her. It was funny. She looked kind of shocked to see a cab instead of a limo. Anyway, she gets in, says, 'How's your daughter?' And they talked about his daughter and her problems with romance the whole trip. So it was almost like reading one of her columns."

"Cool."

"You want to see where she lived? It's on East Lake Shore Drive, the richest street in town."

"For sure."

Ten minutes later I pointed to Ann Landers' old building. "These are all million dollar condos and co-ops," I said. "Like millions and millions. And here, wanna see something cool?" I drove down the block and nosed into the last driveway.

"What's this?" Laura said

"Wait," I said, as the doorman stepped out. I handed him a folded five. "I'm showing my daughter around town," I said. "You mind?"

He smiled and pocketed the bill. "Make sure you wait until it stops," he said. He hit the switch and the turntable turned us around.

"Oh, my god," Laura said. "I want one."

We went north to the Gold Coast, past the old Playboy mansion--now cut up into condos--and then up the street to take a look at the Cardinal's grand residence. "The pope stayed here back in the '70s," I said.

"Bet they had more fun down the street," Laura said.

We headed into Old Town where there were plenty of people waving. "It's a friendly old town," I said.

"Can we pick somebody up?" Laura said.

"Let's see what we can find," I said. "But you gotta at least say hello, okay?"

I passed up several large groups and a couple of young guys, and finally stopped for a businessman with an overcoat and a briefcase. "Ten to one he's going to the train station," I said, and won the bet before the door closed.

"Union Station," he said. "I'm trying to make the 10:40."

"No problem," I said, and Laura popped up and gave him a quick hello.

"Well, hello there, young lady. Now what would you be doing here?"

"I'm just showing her around town," I said.

"Beautiful," the guy said. "I admire your entrepreneurial spirit, sir. And what's the going rate?"

"What's that?"

"A sport gets in, says, 'Where's the action?' You say, 'Funny you should ask.' It's quite a scheme."

"Buddy, stop before you go too far," I said.

He waved some bills in front of Laura. "How much to see your titties, girl? I love fresh young tits."

I laid on the brakes and was out of the cab before he finished the sentence. I jerked the passenger door open but he was already out the other door running, the money still in his hand. He'd left his briefcase behind. I tossed it into oncoming traffic and got back behind the wheel.

Laura was far back in the corner of her seat, her knees to her chest. Her face was pale. Her eyes flat. "Sorry about that," I said, and put the car in gear. We went down a few blocks. "You okay?" I asked, and pulled to the side.

"It was my own fault," she said in a very small voice.

"The guy's a creep. How's that your fault?"

"I'm the one who wanted to pick somebody up."

"Laura, you didn't do anything but say hello. He's the one with the dirty mind."

"I guess so."

"There's no guessing about it," I said. "I'm the one who should have known better."

"Thanks," she said with that same soft voice, and she stayed back in her corner, her feet up on the seat.

FOURTEEN

I started for Ace's then changed my mind and took the highway south, following signs for the Skyway to Indiana.

"This is that road you remember," I said, once we were on the high bridge over the Southeast Side.

"Oh."

The sky was dark. "Most of the steel mills are gone now," I said, and I pointed out smoke rising from a few of the stacks. There were no flames in sight.

We took the last exit to Chicago and drove across 106th Street and into Indiana for cheap gas and Indiana lottery tickets.

"What would you do if you won?" Laura asked after we scratched a few losers.

"I'd never drive a cab again, I'll tell you that much."

"But you like driving."

"Well, yeah, I mean, you gotta work, right? So it's the best of a bad world. So if I won, well, you know one thing I'd like to do? I'd like to drive around and give everybody free rides."

"That'd be so cool."

"But not the rich folks or their punk kids, or that asshole just now. That's the problem with this business. We're usually picking up the wrong people. I'd like to drive out through the neighborhoods and pick up all those poor saps

55

freezing to death at the bus stops. And the ladies with four little kids and a shopping cart struggling to get the groceries home. And the guy walking miles from his job at midnight because the CTA cut his bus route and he doesn't make enough to buy a car. Yeah, all the people who never took a cab in their life. That's who I'd like to give free rides to. The people who could really use one."

"That'd be great."

"So what about you? What would you do if you won?"

She had to think about it. "Travel," she said after a while. "Somewhere I could practice my French. Paris, I guess. But, you know, I'm starting to believe mom. She says money doesn't buy happiness."

"Yeah. She's right, of course. But I'll tell you one thing, she never said that around me. She wanted every penny she could get her little hands on. "

"She said she was the happiest when she was struggling. You know after you left."

"I didn't leave. She threw me out."

"She said that was the best time in her life. Because she was working so hard to pay the bills and keep the house going. And she woke up every morning ready to go out and do whatever she had to."

"Sure. It's like when I found the cab. I was so happy to be making money again. And to realize that I'd always make money as long as there was a cab for me to drive. But I'd still like to win the lottery, Cookie. It's like Ace says, 'I've been rich and I've been poor. Rich is better.' "

"Cookie? Where did that come from?"

"Did I call you that? I didn't even hear it."

"Cookie?"

"There used to be this bakery on Milwaukee Avenue, Polish place. They made these tiny cookies with fruit inside. You loved 'em. You were just learning to talk and that was one of your first words. Cookie. So I used to call you that sometimes. It drove your mother nuts. She didn't like Mary had a little lamb, either."

"You know, I sort of remember you singing that."

"From your initials," I said. "Laura Amber Miles. I used to call you my little lamb. That drove your mother nuts, too."

"I can kind of see why," Laura said. "It doesn't work anymore, anyway."

"No. You're definitely too old."

"And Dan adopted me, so it's not my name."

"Oh, Jesus." That stopped me.

"I was just a kid..."

"It's okay. I deserve it. I mean, he was raising you."

"Not very well," she said.

"I hate to say it. But seems to me you turned out pretty good."

"You don't know what he did," she said, and looked down at her hands.

"He did something to you?"

"Sort of," she said.

"You're gonna have to do better than that."

"It's hard," she said.

"I can't even think about him touching you."

"It was worse than that," she said in a very small voice.

I felt my stomach turn. *Could I bear to hear this?* "Tell me," I said.

"Will you promise to be on my side?"

"Laura, I'm always going to be on your side. Always. No matter what."

A minute or two passed. "I can't figure out how..." She stopped and more time passed. "Can we talk tomorrow? Would that be okay?"

"Sure," I said, and I could feel myself squirming in the seat. "Let's give it a day. Just one day. How's that? One day and then we'll talk."

"Okay," she said, and she sounded as relieved as I was. "Deal."

"Deal," I said, and we bumped fists. "So what's your new name? No. Never mind. You'll always be Laura Miles to me."

"That's kind of how I feel too."

On the way back, at the very top of the Skyway, one of the last steel mills shot a plume of fire straight into the night sky.

Neither one of us said a word.

FIFTEEN

The next afternoon I found one of Laura's gloves on the sidewalk in front of Ace's house. It was powder blue and puffy, full of some miracle space-age insulation that would keep your fingers warm to eighty below.

I went up the stairs wagging the glove in my hand, all set for a bit of fake parental outrage. "Do you think gloves grow on trees? Do you know how hard I had to work to pay for these? And if you're gonna lose a glove"--this from a cabdriver with a trunk loaded with mismatched gloves--"why not do everyone a favor and lose `em both?"

I rang the bell and then opened the storm door. The inside door was ajar. I pushed it and went in. "Laura? Ace?" I called, but no one answered.

I went down the hall to Laura's room. "Baby?" The couch was still open into a bed. But the bed had been stripped. The pillows and covers were in a balled-up mess by the windows. "Laura?" I peeked in the bathroom. A tube of toothpaste sat on top of the sink. A toothbrush lay in the bowl.

I went from one end of the first floor to the other without finding a soul then started upstairs. "Ace, it's Eddie," I called. But no one answered.

About halfway up, a cell phone and a leather slipper lay on the carpeted landing. The upstairs was dark except for a stream of light spilling from a bedroom doorway. "Ace? Laura?"

The bed had been slept in. The covers were thrown back. I walked in and there was Ace, face down on the floor on the far side of the bed, one arm stretched out in front of him. He was barefoot, dressed in pajamas.

"Ace!" I knelt down next to him.

He didn't move or answer. The only sound was the echo of my own voice. I touched the bald spot on the top of his head. It was as cold as ice.

I suddenly heard Laura's voice. *Daddy, don't let them take me.*

Them. My ex and her new husband, the drug-dealing ex-cop who could do anything he wanted and always get away with it.

Blood rushed to my head. I sat down on the bed.

My foot brushed Ace's leg and I let out a groan. "Laura!" I shouted.

I regained my balance and walked downstairs and into Laura's room, calling her name as I went. I opened the closet door. It was completely empty. Everything was gone.

SIXTEEN

The police arrived before too long. I held the door for the first two and pointed the way, then went between them up the stairs. The lead was 35 or so with an oversized gut held in place by a belt loaded with equipment. He took off his hat as he entered the bedroom, then stopped several feet shy of Ace's body and moved to the side.

Cop number two walked past. She was a bit younger than her partner, tall and thin, with curly red hair that peeked out from beneath her cap. She crouched over Ace and held her hand in front of his mouth, then touched the back of his neck. She looked towards her partner and nodded.

"So what happened here?" the partner asked, and he gestured for me to follow him downstairs. Behind us cop number two spoke into a radio.

"Somebody kidnapped my daughter."

"Who's that?" He pointed upstairs.

"Ace," I said. "Carl Rosen. He lives here."

"So what happened to him?"

"He must have tried to stop them."

"How about your daughter. Where's she live?"

"Here. We've been trying to find an apartment."

"You live here, too?"

I shook my head.

"How'd you get in?"

"The door was open."

"You just walked in?"

"I rang the bell," I said. "Nobody answered. Then I came in."

"You just walked into the house?"

"My daughter was staying here."

"You got some ID?"

I handed over my driver's license. "About my daughter?" I said.

"You can explain all that to the sergeant. He should be here any minute."

The sergeant was at least six-four, white hair, pale skin, thin as a rail. He held a quick conference with the two cops then started up the stairs.

On the way, he stopped and took a quick look at the cell phone and the slipper then continued on.

The sergeant stayed upstairs for several minutes. On the way down, he picked up the cell phone, spent a few seconds fiddling with it, then came my way.

He handed me my driver's license.

"Thanks."

"This yours?" He held up the cell phone.

"I think that's . . ." I pointed upstairs.

"You got a key to this place by any chance?"

"Yeah." Ace had given me one the night Laura arrived.

He looked toward the beat men and gave them a slight shrug. "You mind showing my boys how it works, put their minds at ease."

I put the key into the lock and clicked it a few times. He gave the two cops another look.

"So what's this about your daughter," the sergeant asked. "You think somebody kidnapped her?"

"My ex," I said. "Probably along with her husband. He's an . . . well some kind of tough guy according to my daughter."

"So this is a custody thing?" the sergeant asked.

I shook me head. "She's eighteen."

"Look, I'm gonna try to get the dicks out on this. But I gotta warn you. They're not gonna want to waste a lot of time with some battle between you and your ex."

"Even if they killed him?"

"I gotta say it looks like a natural to me. No blood. No smell of gunpowder. No sign of a struggle. Face down on the floor. That's pretty classic. Did he have heart problems by any chance?"

"He had something a few years back," I said. "That's why he retired. I know they told him not to shovel the snow."

He gave me the same look he'd given the beat cops earlier.

An ambulance pulled up. "Hang tight," the sergeant said, and went out to meet them. The ambulance crew had a stretcher half out when the sergeant walked up. They pushed it back, closed the door, and then they all walked inside and up the stairs.

They weren't long. They came down and the ambulance guys went out, got back in the ambulance and drove away. The sergeant talked into his radio then came my way.

"They say natural, too," the sergeant said. "That's just a guess, of course. They're not docs. But he's got a bump on his forehead--probably hit the dresser on the way down--and that's enough to call it a possible homicide. Dicks should be here before too long. What do you know about next of kin?"

"He's got a couple of daughters."

"You know their names?"

I shook my head. I'd said hello to them at his wife's funeral. That was it.

He fiddled with the cell phone for a while. "Marilyn," he said. "That sound familiar?"

"Not really."

"How about Irene?"

"Yeah," I said. "That's one of 'em. He used to sing that song sometimes. `Good night Irene.'"

"I'll get you in my dreams," the sergeant said, then turned to the beat cops. "Why don't you guys go hide somewhere. I'll hang out for the dicks."

The beat cops started away.

"Wait." The cops stopped. "How about one black coffee for me and one..." The sergeant pointed at me.

"Cream," I said.

"And one with cream for Mr. Miles here." He held out a five dollar bill.

"We got it, Sarge," the woman said. The sergeant put his money away.

"So where'd you go to high school?" the sergeant asked after the others were gone.

"Weber."

"They had a hell of a football team way back when. Hey, do you think your friend would mind if we got comfortable while we waited?"

"I'm sure he wouldn't," I said, and I followed him

63

into the living room.

"Was he a smoker by any chance?"

SEVENTEEN

The sergeant smoked and we drank coffee and talked high school sports, this, that, and the other thing, until the detectives arrived.

"You know the only thing worse than an ex-wife?" the sergeant asked.

"Maybe having her kidnap your daughter," I said.

He gave me a long look then pointed to himself. "Three ex-wives. You still pushing a hack, Eddie?"

I took a closer look. "You the guy gave me that speeding ticket?"

He smiled and shook his head. "I haven't written a ticket in twenty years," he said. "William Calloway. That ring any bells?"

This was the guy who'd killed Polack Lenny. "Hard to forget a guy who tries to kill you," I said. But the sergeant still didn't look familiar. "Were you involved with that?"

"A bit," he said, and the doorbell rang. I moved to get up. The sergeant waved me back down. "These are smart boys. They'll figure it out."

They did. Two middle-aged men in dark suits. One had eyes to match. "Billy boy," he said to the sergeant. "You look relaxed."

"Never better," the sergeant said. "This is Mr. Edwin Miles. Goes by Eddie. Friend of the deceased, one Carl Rosen, who you will find upstairs in the master bedroom."

"Nicest guy in the world," the sergeant said after

the detectives left the room. "But he's got the scariest looking eyes. Did you notice?"

I said I had. They were a dull black, without a hint of light or emotion.

"You can't lie to those eyes."

"I'm not planning to."

"You're a little edgy, Eddie. Am I imagining things?"

"Sarge, someone kidnapped my daughter."

"See, you want these guys to help on the daughter angle, you gotta relax a bit. They're nice guys. But, you know, they're dicks, which means they're prima donnas. You start lying to them or trying to pressure them, they're either gonna turn it around on you or disappear. Trust me on this. I've seen it happen."

"So what am I supposed to do?"

"Just answer their questions. Don't ask any. Think you can do that?"

"I'll try."

"So Billy," the Dead-eyed detective said not more than two minutes later, "where's this possible homicide we heard about?"

"Natural death," the sergeant said. "That's exactly what I told Mr. Miles here. Ain't that right? And it turns out the guy had a bad ticker to boot."

"So why are we here?"

"Well, the ambulance guys saw a bump and they made it a possible homicide. And I figured you guys wouldn't mind taking a look, especially if I left him right where he landed instead of having him transported all the way up to St. Francis."

"The *ambulance crew?* Now why do I think there's something else going on?"

"Right you are. See, Mr. Miles here has an 18-year-old daughter, name of Laura. She was staying in the guest room." The sergeant pointed that way. "She's gone along with all her possessions, except for a single glove which was found on the parkway outside." Once again, he pointed the way.

"The father here feels his daughter might have been kidnapped, possibly by the ex-wife. Now I know what you're thinking. But there's a couple of extenuating circumstances. Number one: the girl came cross-country from California on a Greyhound bus barely a week ago. Number two: Mr. Miles here had not seen little Laura in almost ten years. That's when he lost custody. But he never once tried to kidnap the girl. Number three: Mr. Miles is not related to the mayor or a single alderman. He has no high-ranking friends within the Chicago Police Department. But he did help out on a case a few years back, and I feel we owe him a little something in return.

"Now I don't want to hang you up here, fellows. I know you've probably got places to go, things to do. And I've already got a couple of numbers for next of kin. So I can handle all that. I got 'em off the victim's--I'm sorry--off the deceased's phone here. Filed right under In Case of Emergency. ICE. You gotta love that, right?"

"Okay, Billy," Dead-eye said, "we'll be going now. Thanks for the entertainment."

The sergeant tossed the cell phone. Dead-eye caught it one-handed. "What am I supposed to do with this?"

"I thought you might like to see the last number

Mr. Rosen dialed."

Dead eye fiddled with the phone for a moment. "He was having a heart attack. He called 9-1-1."

"Now if I was having a heart attack," the sergeant said, "and it probably won't be long now, and I had enough time to dial 9-1-1, why would I go up to the bedroom? Wouldn't I want to go down to wait for the ambulance?"

"Hell, he wanted to lie down," Dead-eye said. "That don't make it a homicide."

"You know, I was thinking he might have been going upstairs for some kind of medicine," the sergeant said. "Did you happen to look in that nightstand? It almost looks like that's where he was heading."

EIGHTEEN

"You're telling me you don't know your own daughter's name?"

This was Dead-eye, also known as Detective Mulvey. He was now sitting on Ace's sofa with a notebook open on the coffee table in front of him. Next to the notebook was the Browning .45 caliber automatic pistol that had been found in the drawer of Ace's nightstand, fully loaded and ready to go. USMC was stenciled on both hand grips. It had been passed from cop to cop several times. The consensus was that Ace had somehow smuggled the weapon home from Korea.

"Her stepfather adopted her somewhere along the line. But to me she's Laura Miles," I said. "But I know that doesn't help you any."

"This means you also don't know your ex-wife's

new name?"

"Yeah. Sorry," I said. "I know her maiden name."

"Okay. Hit me."

"Keating," I said. "Susan Keating."

Dead-eye scribbled in his notebook. "Hard to believe," he said.

"I wish I could forget my ex's names," the sergeant said. "Pretty damn hard when you're writing 'em checks every frigging month."

"You know, Billy. You can take off any time. We've got this covered," Dead-eye said.

"Hell, I got nothing better to do," Sergeant Billy said. "I thought I'd do the notification for you, these clowns ever get him out of here."

The clowns showed up in a battered mini van, two kids dressed all in white. That's if you didn't count the numerous tattoos, various body piercings, and fingernails painted black and blue.

I could almost see them, not too long ago, a couple of normal kids admiring their first tattoos. Now they were hauling out the dead. "See what happens." I wanted to tell Laura. But she was nowhere around.

"See where privatization leads," the sergeant said. In the old days, a few years back, the Police Department had carted the bodies away.

He followed the kids upstairs.

"So where do you know Billy from?" Dead-eye asked.

"I'm not sure," I said.

"Oh, that's a good one," Doran said. "Tell us another."

"And you can't even give us an educated guess

where your ex might be living," Dead-eye said. "I mean California is sort of big."

"Somewhere around Los Angeles," I said. "Laura said something about the valley. But I don't know which valley."

Dead-eye was looking at the notebook as if he wanted to write but couldn't find any words. "Now you've known the deceased for years. Did he keep valuables around? Is there something we should make sure is not missing?"

"You know, I was only in the house a couple of times until this week."

"He was in a cash business. Anywhere he might have hidden the loot?"

"He's been retired almost two years," I said.

"It's kind of funny. Besides the cell phone and the slipper, there's no sign of a disturbance. The door's not forced. Place isn't tossed. Only thing missing is your daughter and her stuff. Leads you to believe that she left under her own power. And, you know, if this turns out to be a homicide, right now she would be suspect number one."

"Oh, come on," I said.

"Maybe she grabbed a twenty from your friend and he caught her," Dead-eye said.

The sergeant's voice came from upstairs: "And then he runs up here to get his gun so he can shoot her before she gets away with it."

A minute later, the sergeant came down the stairs followed by the kids in white. They were struggling with an oversized plastic bag with handles on both ends. The sergeant held the door for them. "What do you guys do if you get a normal-size person?" he said, and closed the door behind them.

"Any suggestions?" Dead-eye asked when the sergeant entered the room.

"You know what I'd do if I was you?" the sergeant said. "I'd go to one of those high school reunion sites and I would pretend that I was a girl who graduated from . . ." He pointed my way.

"Madonna High School," I said.

"Back about . . ."

"Oh seventy-eight, seventy-nine," I said.

"And I'll bet you dimes to donuts that somewhere in the last ten years, Susan Keating got lonely for the old home town and, if nothing else, you'll find her new name. Now I know I'm just an old broken down homicide dick who made the mistake of taking the sergeants' test one day."

"Bet it don't feel too bad come pay day," Detective Doran said.

"Yeah, but the fun, boys. The fun. I mean even a case like this. It looks like nothing but trouble. But you play your cards right, you might get a trip to California out of it. In February. My god, why did I ever give this up?"

I stood on the front steps with the sergeant and watched the detectives drive away. "What now?" I said.

"Well, I'm going to make the notification. Unless you want to do it."

"I'll pass," I said.

"Why don't you make sure everything's locked up tight," the sergeant said.

I took a slow walk through the house, making sure the windows and doors were locked. There was a rec room in the basement, with the classic wood paneling, a four-stool bar, and a jukebox. A whole group of us had watched the Bears getting creamed in the Super Bowl down here. I stopped to look at the songs on the jukebox. It was mostly rock and roll from back when Ace's daughters were kids. For some reason, this nearly brought me to tears.

The sergeant was in his squad car talking on the phone. I locked the front door then walked around the side of the house into the yard. The back gate was standing open. I closed it then unlocked the garage with another key I'd gotten from Ace. The Toyota was sitting there in the dark.

Out front, the sergeant was leaning against his squad car. "Marilyn ended up with both sets of keys," he said. "And she's out of town. I told Irene we'd hang out until she gets here. She's just up in Lincolnwood. What say we go talk to the neighbors?"

All we found was a woman who'd seen a young girl, provocatively dressed, leading various older men into Ace's house. "Nothing worse than an old lady with a dirty mind," the sergeant said.

"You said something about William Calloway," I said. This was the guy who'd killed Polack Lenny and then picked me as his next victim.

He smiled. "William Lincoln Calloway, killed your friend Leonard Something-or-another, right?"

"Smigelkowski," I said. "We called him Polack Lenny."

"I was still a detective back then," he said. "I had the Indian cabbie."

"The one in Old Town?" I said and the sergeant

nodded. He'd been killed about a week before Lenny.

"Raj Chopra," the sergeant said, and he held his thumb and index finger an inch apart. "He was about this fucking big. He came here to be a doctor and ended up driving a hack for thirty years. But he put every one of his kids through college and two of 'em ended up docs themselves. His wife was old country but the kids were as American as you and me. I wasn't getting anywhere on it. Nowhere. And for some reason I really, really wanted it. And then some cabbie name of Eddie Miles comes along and clears my case for me. Yeah. I figure I owe you."

"Luckiest day of my life," I said.

"You make your own luck in this world," he said, and his radio spoke. "Duty calls," he said a minute later. "You mind hanging out and opening the door?"

"No problem," I said. "Thanks for your help."

"By any chance are you working later tonight?"

"I don't know," I said. "I don't know what I'm gonna do." I couldn't even think about driving a cab right now. "Why?"

"Well, me and the current are heading out to Vegas for a long weekend. I live out in Edison Park. It would give us a bit more time to talk."

"What time?"

"We should be at O'Hare at five in the morning."

"Pick you up at four-thirty, how's that sound?"

"That would be lovely, Eddie. Just lovely," he said and gave me his address. "Come in off of Northwest Highway."

NINETEEN

Ace's daughter Irene and her son Steve pulled up in a shiny Volvo station wagon. She was older than me but you'd never guess it. She looked fit and sexy in a corduroy jacket, blue jeans, and well-polished boots. The sparkle in her eyes reminded me of Ace. Even her hair glowed.

"I'm really sorry about your father," I said. "He was a great guy."

"Eddie, I've been hearing about you for years." She extended her hand and I took it. "Dad always said he wanted to go quickly." She had a nice firm grip.

"Yeah," I said. "I remember that." Ace's wife had lingered for months.

"This is my son Steve," Irene said.

"Hey," I said and extended my hand. "Nice to meet you."

He muttered something. His hand felt a bit like a creampuff. He was probably in his mid-twenties, overweight and pale, with acne and too much hair. He looked like the kind of kid who never moved out of his parent's basement. But I could tell that Irene didn't see any of that.

She put her hand on his shoulder and we walked up the steps. I unlocked the door, slid the key off the ring and handed it over.

"Do you have another for yourself?"

"No."

"You should. Does Laura have one?"

73

"She's gone," I said.

"She left?" I nodded. "Steven, would you put the kettle on, please."

The kid went towards the kitchen and Irene and I walked upstairs and I pointed out the spot where Ace had fallen. She grabbed my arm and held on for a long moment. "Oh, dad," she said.

I didn't notice the stains on the floor until she went into the bathroom and came back with a damp towel. She crouched down over the spot where Ace had lain. She was still for a minute or two then she went down on one knee and wiped the stains away. She stood up, puffed out the pillow, and pulled the covers over it.

"My dad really liked your daughter," she said as we walked downstairs. "Where did she go? Was she here?"

I shook my head. "I don't know," I said. "She disappeared."

She led me into the kitchen. The tea kettle was on the burner but her son was nowhere around. "Sit," she said. "Let me make you some tea." The sound of music came from downstairs. "Steve can't wait to get that jukebox home," she said. "That's his big inheritance."

We sat at the kitchen table, sipping tea, and I told her the entire story.

"The police told me they thought he'd had a heart attack," she said when I was finished.

"Well, I guess he did," I said. "But what brought it on. That's what I'd like to know. I'm pretty sure he was going for that gun. Why else would he run upstairs?"

"I found that one day when I was a girl," she said. "I was home from school sick and my mother went shopping or something, so I was searching the house, trying to find whatever the adults hid from the children. That was the most shocking thing I ever found. It was in that nightstand. Always. But there were times when I'd hear some noise late at night and it was a comfort to know my father was down the hall with his gun."

"You know, I didn't even know he was in Korea until the other day."

"I think he was embarrassed," she said. "He grew up with all these tough Jews on the old West Side. He wanted to be refined. But then his father died and Dad had to quit school and go to work in a foundry to help support the family. He was relieved when he got drafted. He knew it'd be easier work than the foundry."

"He got drafted into the Marines?"

"He used to tell that story. The Marines were short their quota for the month so they picked the three guys at the end of the line and said, 'You. You and you. This way. You're Marines.'"

"And he ended up a cabdriver," I said.

"He was embarrassed by that too," she said. "His father was a knife sharpener. Do you remember those? He had a horse and wagon and he rode up and down the street sharpening knives. He had a heart attack, too, and then the horse carried him all the way home. When dad was down in the dumps about driving a cab he'd say at least his father had a horse to keep him company."

75

TWENTY

My apartment was too clean. I missed the old dump. But any cave would do. I crawled in, locked the door behind me, and pulled down the shades.

My phone started ringing, one cabdriver after another. It rang more and more as the night went on. It was after ten when I finally got enough energy to answer.

"Eddie, where the hell are you?" Ken Willis asked. "You heard about Ace, right?"

"Yeah."

"Well, where are you? Everybody's at the roundtable."

"I'll be by in a while," I said.

"Bring your girl," he said. "Was she there when it happened?"

"I'm not sure."

"Why don't you ask her?"

"She's gone."

"Gone where?"

"I don't know," I said and disconnected the call.

It wasn't long before my doorbell was ringing. I ignored it. But, like any other toilet, there was little in the way of security at the Rosewood Arms, and soon there was a pounding on the door. "Come on, Eddie. Open up. It's Ken."

He was ready to start pounding again when I caught him with his arm in the air. "Jesus Christ," he said. "Are you okay?"

"Of course, I'm not okay. How could I be okay?"

"So what happened?"

"Somebody took her."

"Who?"

"My ex, I guess."

"Did you call the police?"

"Yes. I called the police."

"What'd they say?"

"It's a fucking joke to them. They don't give two shits about her or about Ace for that matter. This one cop, I thought he was trying to help. You know what it's about? He wants a free ride to O'Hare for his long weekend in Vegas."

"Well, fuck him, right?"

"Yeah. Except he was the one who figured out about the gun. So maybe he's right. Maybe I do owe him."

"What gun?"

"Ace's," I said. "That's what he was trying to get to."

"Eddie, could I come in?"

TWENTY-ONE

I washed my face and put on a fresh shirt. We went downstairs and I slid into the front seat next to Ken and we headed for the roundtable.

"You sure you don't want to pick up your cab?" Ken asked.

"I don't think I'll ever drive again," I said. *Would I ever see Laura again?*

"You know how many times I've said that? What else you gonna do?"

"Just something different," I said. "There's gotta be something more interesting than driving around in circles."

"Now you're sounding like Ace." This was one of his standard raps; how he'd wasted his life driving in circles. And now it was over. *Had it really been a waste?*

They were holding the cabdriver's wake in the back room of the Golden Batter Pancake House on Lincoln Avenue. We all called it the roundtable, although there wasn't a round table in the entire place.

When Ken and I walked in, it made an even dozen. This was the largest turnout in years. But there were several drivers missing.

Polack Lenny had been murdered for a couple of hundred bucks. Roy Davidson had had a stroke on the way to O'Hare. He'd managed to get off the highway and drive himself and his passengers to the emergency room at Resurrection Hospital. He'd made it another year, hobbling around with two canes. But that was his last load.

Herb Jones had been broadsided by a brand new Porsche doing 110 on Christmas night. Alex was now a high school gym teacher. He'd been going to college for years without ever letting on. Tony Golden had sold his medallion and used the proceeds to expand his minor real estate empire. Tony still hung around the roundtable. Alex stopped by now and then.

"Ace was the last of the World War Two guys," Escrow Jake said as we joined the crowd.

"Was he that old?" a guy I didn't recognize said.

"Korea," I said as we sat down. "He showed me his tattoo the other day."

This brought shouts of "Ace had a tattoo?" from

half the table.

"He was in the Marines," I said.

More shouts: "Ace was a Marine?"

"And it might not have been a heart attack that killed him," Ken Willis said, and the whole place shut up.

As Ken filled everybody in, I demolished a ham and cheese omelet without tasting anything.

"Ace was having a great time with Laura," the guy I didn't know said. "He told me he hoped you never found an apartment." *Who was this guy?*

"The thing about Ace," someone said, and they were off to the races.

"Look, Ace is dead," Ken Willis interrupted after a while. "And that's too bad and everything. But Ace was an old man. He wasn't gonna be around long, no matter what. Laura's a kid and she's alive. So the question is: How do we get her back?"

He might as well have asked how we could get our taxis to fly. And I probably looked as clueless as everyone else.

"Eddie, you gotta go to California," Escrow Jake said. "It's that simple."

"And do what? I don't even know her name."

"Do you know your ex's social security number," Tony Golden asked.

"I could probably find it," I said. "I've got a box with divorce papers and stuff like that. But what good will that do?"

"I run credit checks all the time for my apartments," Golden said. "You get all sorts of information. It only costs about eighty-five bucks. You get bankruptcies and evictions, criminal records. All sorts of things."

"I still don't see what good that does," I said.

"Well, if the other guy adopted Laura that might show up."

"On a credit check, come on?"

"Eddie, I'm trying to help."

"Sorry," I said. "You know this cop had an idea how to find her." And I told them the sergeant's high school reunion idea. "Any of you guys got a computer?"

Almost everybody did.

"I saw something on TV a while back," the guy I didn't know said. "These Mormons run these wilderness camps out in the middle of nowhere. They're kind of like re-education camps for kids running wild, you know drugs and sex or whatever. And if the kids won't go voluntarily, the Mormons send these huge Samoans to kidnap 'em. I mean Laura's a tough kid and everything but she's probably not strong enough to overcome a couple of Samoan wrestlers trying to stuff her into a bag."

I had a sudden picture of Ace going out the door in his plastic bag.

"Who the fuck are you?" I said. "You don't even know her."

There was a silence around the table and then the guy said, "Sorry, Eddie, you're right. I'm Wesley. I'm the guy who . . ."

"Oh, for Christsake," I said. Here was the driver who had found Laura at the Greyhound station. I walked down to shake his hand. "I've been meaning to look you up, to thank you for everything. Now what was that you were saying?"

"Oh, just talking out my ass," he said. "Something I saw on TV."

"Tell me again," I said. It had been in the back of my mind all day. Why hadn't Laura put up a struggle? Maybe they'd found her asleep. A couple of huge Samoans with a big black bag. The one I saw in my mind had handles on each end.

TWENTY-TWO

The closet had once held a Murphy bed. It was double-door wide but not very deep, and hadn't been opened in years. I pushed the sofa out of the way, opened one door then the other, and found a crumpled cardboard box down in a corner. "Misc. Papers," was written in black. I pulled it out and something fell.

Laura's scrapbook.

For years, I'd cut photographs out of newspapers, pictures that reminded me of Laura. News stories. Things I thought she might like.

As her birthday approached, I'd start searching for the perfect present. She'd always end up with more than one, sometimes four or five. Pictures of presents came pretty cheap, of course. *But why had I stopped?*

I put the carton on the kitchen table then picked up the scrapbook and turned to the first page.

"12-YEAR-OLD WINS SPELLING BEE."

It was a small story but for some reason it had caught my eye. A twelve-year old girl in New Jersey had won a spelling bee by correctly spelling *etymology.* I flipped through the book. There were more cut-out newspaper stories and loads of pictures; young girls modeling clothes or competing in athletics or science fairs.

I'd kept the book for five years, from the time she was twelve until she was sixteen. Why had I stopped?

I flipped to the end. I'd picked a single present for her 16th birthday, a Beetle convertible, as yellow as sunshine. But there weren't any news stories, just some pictures of girls playing volleyball and basketball.

The news had turned grim that year; sixteen-year-old girls charged in killings and arrested in drug busts; girls forced into the sex trade; girls raped and murdered.

But that wasn't it. It was the car. That's why I'd stopped.

If she were real, I'd realized, I would never buy her a convertible. What kind of father would get his daughter a car without a roof? But since she wasn't real it didn't matter. None of it mattered. I'd been kidding myself for years.

I put the scrapbook away and started digging through the carton, looking for my ex's social security number. It didn't take long to get side-tracked. The first detour was our wedding album. Quite a few pictures were missing, mostly from Susan's side of the family. Had she taken them or had I thrown them out? It didn't matter, I decided. There wasn't a single person in the album that I was still in touch with.

My birth certificate from Ft. Wayne floated to the top. I'd spent all of six months there and had never bothered to return. A bill from the funeral home four years after my mother had been deposited next to my father. "If the past due amount is not paid immediately this matter will be promptly turned over for collection!" If I'd ever heard from the collection agency, I didn't remember. Had I actually paid the bill?

My report card from fourth grade. "If Edwin does not improve his attitude he will not get far." The teacher's name was at the bottom of the card but I didn't remember her. I could barely remember where we'd lived that year. But the real mystery was who had saved the card and why.

There was a bundle of World War II letters from the man I'd been named after, my father's older brother Edwin. He'd died at 22 in France a few months before the end of the war. My father had rarely talked about him and never mentioned the war. I'd read the letters over and over again when I was in high school. But they weren't any more forthcoming than my father. It was nothing but small talk.

I got up and started pacing and the apartment got smaller and smaller. What the hell was I doing driving myself crazy? I opened a shade and looked down to Montrose Avenue. The bus wouldn't be running for an hour or two. But I could see the reflection of the lights from the late-night saloon down the street. A cab shot past. A passenger in the back seat was holding a lit cigarette out a partially open window.

It was a half mile walk down Montrose to Welles Park and Western Avenue, where the cab was parked and waiting. I pulled out, headed north on

Western, and there was a slight guy teetering and swaying in the breeze.

I wasn't sure if he wanted a cab or not. But when I stopped for the light, he opened the door. "Straight up to Peterson," he said.

"You getting out on the corner?"

"What's wrong with this city?" he shouted.

"Buddy, I just woke up," I said. "Give me a break, huh?"

"You got any music?" he asked a couple of minutes later.

"Radio doesn't work." If I turned it on, he'd want one station after another until the perfect song came along. By the time it arrived, we'd be at his destination.

We passed a defrocked Yellow Cab with a broken mirror parked a bit cockeyed alongside the cemetery. The medallion and decals were gone. Parking tickets were fluttering on the windshield.

"Right here," the guy said a block later.

"Five-twenty," I said.

He handed me a ten. "Your lucky night," he said.

I continued north and then turned left on Ace's block. It was just another dark house. Nobody was sitting on the porch. I drove around back, parked in the alley with my flashers going, got out, opened the gate, and walked into the yard.

The curtains were wide open. The hide-a-bed was back to being a sofa. I tapped lightly on a window. "Laura," I called. No one answered.

I headed back south and nothing was shaking. I switched over to Lincoln, heading southeast. I was the only car in sight. Past Irving Park a couple of empty cabs passed going in the other direction. These were usually the hardest hours to get through. The bars were mostly closed. The city was sleeping. But there was always someone who needed a cab. And you wouldn't find them unless you went looking.

That was the one great thing about the cab business. It was always there. So when you had nothing else in the world, when you'd let them take your daughter--or you'd given her away--you could drive and drive and pretend you were actually getting somewhere.

More than once I'd heard Ken Willis compare cab driving to a long night on the town. "You spend your night talking to a bunch of strangers but when you wake up the next day it's all a blur. You don't remember who anybody was or what anybody said. The big difference, you find a pile of cash in your pocket and you say, 'Where did all this come from?'"

On good days you could tell jokes with your passengers, talk about the weather or the Cubs or the Sox, and pretend that they were friends. And on bad days you could sit in stony silence and hate every one of them.

It took me about fifteen minutes and then there they were----the last of the night people, spilling out of a 24-hour diner. Three of them climbed in. Two stops, the last one put me right at Fullerton and Western, about a block from the highway.

Oh, what the hell, I decided, I might as well go give the sergeant his free ride.

It was about ten minutes up to Edison Park, a

quiet suburban-looking neighborhood loaded with cops, firemen, and other city workers who all had to live within the city.

I got a bit turned around but eventually found the sergeant's street. The porch light flashed the moment I pulled up. A few seconds later the front door opened and the sergeant and his fourth wife started down the stairs. She was a few inches shorter than her husband, which still put her somewhere around six feet. She was a good twenty years younger.

I got out and opened the trunk. "Top of the morning, Eddie," the sergeant said. "This is the lovely missus, Caroline. I've been telling her all about you."

"Hello," I said.

"Nice to meet you," Caroline said. She was a slender brunette with a nice smile.

"Now, Caroline," the sergeant said once we were underway, "I hope you don't mind if we talk a little business."

"Just pretend I'm painting my toenails," she said.

"I talked to my guy at the morgue," the sergeant said. "It's a riot. They're almost out of money. The state stopped ponying up their share. So they're all backed up. They can't even get the paupers buried. How's that for a kick in the pants? And, of course, they're way behind with the autopsies. So the earliest they're gonna get to your friend is next week. And if they don't call it a homicide you're stuck with no action.

"So here." He handed up a business card. "Mike Cantore, ex-cop, ex-choirboy, Eagle Scout, the whole bit, and then he goes over to the dark side. Private peeper. But he's good. And he's fairly straight. And he's got a twelve-year-old hidden in a closet somewhere who is an absolute whiz on a computer. Now if I was you and I wanted to find my little girl, he's the guy I'd call."

"Thanks," I said. I took a quick look at the card, *Michael Cantore Investigations,* and then tucked it away in my shirt pocket. But I could already see myself throwing it out the window.

"Now this is important," the sergeant said. "You don't want to give him too much money. I know for a fact he's hurting. So whatever he asks for offer him half. Tell him that's all you can afford and don't go any higher. He needs the dough."

"Thanks. Should I mention your name?"

"Never. That would be the worst thing you could do. He asks, tell him Mulvey gave you his name. Now he probably hates Mulvey, too. But he's gonna be too afraid to mess with him. Those eyes terrify everybody. Hey, Caroline, what would you think if my eyes were a dull black and reflected no light?"

"Too much Guinness, more than likely."

We were pulling up to the terminals when the sergeant said, "Eddie, you forgot to turn on the meter."

"It's on the house," I said.

"Thanks, Eddie. Didn't I tell you this was a man, Caroline?"

"You did."

"But would that be the way to start a trip to Vegas? Stiff the cabbie. What do you think, honey?"

"A total jinx," Caroline said.

The sergeant handed me a pair of twenties and refused to take change. I got out, opened the trunk, found them a loose luggage cart, and they went skipping into the terminal.

TWENTY-THREE

At home I crawled straight into bed, but barely slept.

Before long, I was back at the kitchen table, going through the box. I found an envelope from my father on Palmer House stationery addressed to my mother back home in Indiana. He'd come to Chicago for a job interview with the commercial printer where he ended up working until he retired. But he was worried about the dirt and chaos of Chicago. "You have to fight the crowds just to get across the street here," he wrote. "We must think about the boys, too." A few years later my older brother was killed by a hit and run driver. My father went to his grave convinced he should never have left Ft. Wayne.

I finally found the envelope with the divorce papers. I scanned them quickly looking for my ex's social security number, then went back through it slowly. I'd never actually gone to court. I'd signed some paper agreeing to the terms and my ex had stood before a judge and answered a series of questions. I was halfway through the six page transcript when the phone rang.

"Eddie?" a woman said.

"Who's this?"

"Look, I wouldn't bother you unless it was important. But has Laura been in touch, by any chance?"

"Who is this?"

"It's Susan. Remember me? We used to be married a long time ago."

"You fucking bitch," I shouted. "What kind of shit are you trying to pull?"

"Eddie!"

"And don't fucking Eddie me you conniving cunt. You took her and I'm getting her back and when I do you will never, ever, see her again."

"Are you drunk?"

"Fuck you," I shouted and I threw the phone across the room.

I looked down at the divorce papers in my hand and realized what I'd just done. "Shit," I said, and I went and found the phone, which was now in pieces. I got it back together and, as soon as I did, it rang.

"Please don't hang up," Susan said.

"Sorry about that," I said.

"Nobody's yelled at me like that in years."

"It was probably me."

"Well, if nothing else, I know exactly where you stand."

"Hey, what's your new name?"

"What new name?"

"Your new husband, didn't you take his name?"

"No. I figured I made that mistake once. I'm good old Susan Keating, just like when we met."

"But you let Laura take his name?"

"Eddie, is she there?"

"Do you really think I'm that stupid?"

"Eddie, just tell me she's okay. Please."

"You were always a great liar."

"Eddie, please. This is important. At first I figured it was just a little snit. She was punishing us because we didn't take her on vacation with us."

"Why you feeding me this bullshit?"

"I'm telling you this because they found her boyfriend dead off Malibu. I've called all of Laura's friends, everyone I could think of, and nobody's seen her. So I'm going crazy hoping your daughter is not out there in the middle of the fucking ocean and you're calling me a cunt. So could you please tell me if you've heard from her? Is that too much to ask? Just tell me she's alive."

"Oh, fuck," I said, and I realized that Laura had lied about calling her mother.

"What?"

"She showed up last week on a Greyhound bus."

"Oh, thank god."

"No," I said. "She disappeared yesterday. I'm pretty sure she was kidnapped. You were my number one suspect."

"Oh, Jesus, Mary and Joseph."

"You sure you didn't have anything to do with it?"

"You haven't changed a bit. You know that? Your own daughter and you can't protect her. Did you ever do one thing right in your entire, worthless, life?"

The phone went dead in my ear.

TWENTY-FOUR

Tony Golden called wondering if I'd found Susan's social security number. I told him that was on hold for the moment and when he pushed for an explanation I told him I had another call.

It wasn't long before one came in. Fat Wally had used his computer to sign up as a Madonna High School grad. "She's still using Susan Keating," he said. "At least for the reunion site. She gave her hometown as Culver City. But no phone and no street address. Just an e-mail."

"Culver City," I said. "Is that in a valley?"

"It looks like it's right where Interstate 10 and Interstate 405 meet."

That didn't mean anything to me. I wrote down the e-mail address and thanked him, and then looked up Susan's number on my phone. "You know the drill," her recorded voice said just before the beep.

I crawled into bed without bothering to undress. I punched in the number again and again as day turned into night. I never left the apartment, never touched the cab. The only answer I got was Susan's voice followed by a beep.

TWENTY-FIVE

"I don't think I've ever been to a Sunday funeral," Ken Willis said. We were in his private car heading west as snow began to fall.

"He's Jewish," I said. "They like to get 'em in the ground right away."

"Sure," Ken said. "Saves on embalming."

The cemetery was off of Madison Street in suburban Forest Park, a couple of miles west of the city limit. "Good thing we came," Ken whispered as we walked up. There weren't twenty people, and that included the grave diggers. There were several kids, and two men as old as Ace who stood holding hands.

There were no real services, just some mumbo-jumbo from a rabbi, then the coffin was lowered into the ground.

We all took turns filling in the grave with earth and snow while the grave diggers lounged in the background.

After my turn, I walked over and said hello to Irene and Marilyn.

"Thank you so much for coming," Irene said. "We know you work nights." She handed me a slip of paper with an address on it. "If you get up near Lincolnwood any time this week, please stop by."

"Oh, sure, thanks," I said. "Hey, how'd you get him out of the morgue? Somebody told me it was going to take forever."

"The funeral director took care of that," she said. "I know it cost a little extra."

"You paid off the morgue?"

She raised an eyebrow. "I believe they called it a gratuity."

"Only in Chicago," I said.

"That's exactly what dad would have said."

"Most of the furniture is going to charity," Marilyn said. "If there's anything you'd like, please let us know."

"Oh, thanks," I said.

"The living room sofa and the jukebox are already spoken for."

TWENTY-SIX

I started dialing Susan's number as soon as I got home. The phone rang and rang. About two o'clock she finally answered.

"Look, we gotta talk," I said.

"Fine. I'm just picking up a rental at O'Hare. I'm staying at the Holiday Inn on Touhy. How about Jack's? Is that still there?"

"I don't have a car," I said. "So what'd you do, fly in?"

"No. I walked and my feet are killing me." But it wasn't a joke. I was the joke. "So where do we meet? Is there a corner Greek joint somewhere?"

Two hours later, I looked out to Irving Park Road from the Alps diner and there she was, bumper parking a red sub-compact. I hadn't seen her in ten long years and I had hoped never to see her again.

She got out and took a look around the neighborhood--with everyone dressed for the dead of winter--and a familiar look of disgust flickered across her face.

I walked outside to greet her. "I don't believe this," I said when she was halfway across the street. She was the brightest object on Irving Park Road and she knew it. Her blond hair framed a glowing sun tan and bounced down to touch the top of a light-weight jacket. *Too bad it's not twenty below.* That'd get that smirk off her face.

She did a little dance. "You miss me, Eddie?"

"You don't look a day older," I said, and it was almost true. She was seven years younger than me which made her 45. But you'd never guess it from her looks.

"You probably don't need me to tell you what you look like," she said, and walked past without a handshake or a hug.

I followed her into the diner and pointed towards the booth where my coffee sat cooling. "You called the police, I take it," she said after her own coffee arrived.

"Of course."

"So what'd they say?" she asked. "Are they looking for her?"

"It's a little more complicated than just Laura missing," I said.

"What the hell does that mean?"

"Take it easy and I'll tell you."

"Okay. The police don't care. I've got that," she said after the food was out of the way. "Now tell me what you've been doing all this time."

"Believe it or not, trying to find your address."

"What were you planning to do with it?"

"I was going to go wherever the hell you're living and make sure Laura was alright."

"Did you ever think of 4-1-1?"

"Okay. I admit it. I'm stupid. I just assumed if you changed Laura's name, you changed your own."

"'Don't let them take me?'"

"That's what she said. Or don't let them take me back."

"It could have been something in a dream she was having."

"Sure."

"So the only cop who might help us is . . ."

94

"The sergeant," I said.

". . . in 'Vegas."

"Till Monday," I said.

"Well, let's go see the other ones."

TWENTY-SEVEN

The police station at Belmont and Western brought back memories. I'd spent several hours in the lockup one night. But there were good memories too. Once upon a time this area had been Riverview, Chicago's biggest and best amusement park. "Laugh your troubles away," the radio shouted all summer long.

We ignored the sign that said, ALL VISITORS MUST CHECK IN, and followed the one that said DETECTIVE DIVISION - SECOND FLOOR. It led us to a big, open squad room with maybe twenty desks and a handful of detectives.

"You see 'em?"

"No." And just then Dead-eye stepped out of a door at the back of the room. "Wait. That's one of 'em. Detective Mulvey."

Dead-eye saw us coming but if he recognized me he gave no sign. Susan stepped right in front of him. "My daughter is missing," she said.

"Tell 'em at the desk downstairs," he said, and tried to move around her. But Susan moved right with him.

"Detective," I said. "Our daughter is the girl who was staying with Carl Rosen."

"Rosen," he said. "We're waiting for the autopsy on that. Try me in a couple of days."

"Detective," Susan blocked his path again. "My daughter is missing. And if you think you're going to get rid of me that easily you are sadly mistaken."

"Lady, I'm in the middle of an interrogation." He pointed towards the room he'd come out of. "I have a suspect in there. An actual suspect in an actual homicide investigation."

"Would it interest you to know that my daughter's boyfriend was murdered in California?" she said and kicked the side of my foot.

"Where was this?" Dead-eye asked.

"Malibu."

"Keep going," Dead-eye said, and there was actually a bit of light in his eyes.

"I don't really know all the details," Susan said.

"How about a name?"

"Scott."

"Is that first or last," Dead-eye asked. "Or was he like Prince?"

"He was found in the ocean," Susan said. "But he didn't drown."

"No? What happened to him?"

"They're even slower there than here," Susan said. "Have you ever thought about contacts?"

"What?"

"For your eyes," she said. "Contact lens. I think they might help. That dark look is so dull. You need a bit of color."

"Is that right?" he said, and he was smiling now, which brought even more light into those eyes.

"Maybe brown," Susan said. "No. Gray. That might make you look very intelligent."

Now his eyes were shining brightly. He barely looked like the same man. "You don't think I look intelligent, Mrs...?"

"Keating. Call me Susan."

"Susan, look," he said, "I'd love to sit down and talk with you and. . ."

"My ex-husband."

"Your ex. But I really am in the middle of something. And it's probably going to go all night. So how about tomorrow at four? That's right when I go on duty. So we'll have plenty of time to talk."

"About my daughter," Susan said.

"I thought you wanted to talk about my eyes."

"They're starting to look almost human," she said. "Is that some kind of trick?"

TWENTY-EIGHT

"Cops," Susan said when we were back in her rent-a-car. "They pretend they're so tough. But once you get past that wall, they're all just little boys."

"I hear you married one," I said.

"So?"

"So the thing about Laura's boyfriend being murdered?"

"I assumed he drowned but now with this, who knows?"

"Here's what bothers me," I said. It had been bothering me ever since Susan had called. "If you didn't take her, who did?"

"God only knows."

"And if it was some pervert, she could be dead by now."

"Don't say that!"

"And you know it too."

"Just don't say it. We can't think that way."

"But maybe it's like Dead-eye says."

"Dead-eye?"

"Detective Mulvey. He said if Ace was murdered, Laura might be the number one suspect."

"The man's an idiot."

"Sure. Probably. But his point was, there was no sign of a struggle. And all her stuff is gone. Everything. That looked so much like you."

"What?"

"Clearing the whole place out. Making sure you didn't leave anything behind. You'd do that. And maybe Laura would do that. But who else? I mean some random pervert; he doesn't care about a closet full of clothes."

"What are you trying to say?"

"Nothing, I guess."

"Then why don't you just shut the fuck up?"

We were stopped for the light at Addison. I opened the door, got out, and leaned back in. "You know, I'm not your fucking husband. And I certainly don't have to worry about losing custody of Laura. So if you can't be polite..." I slammed the door.

She followed along in the curb lane as I walked north up Western Avenue.

"I'm sorry," she called a half block later. "Look, we need each other now. I'm sorry. Please get back in the car."

I got back in and we continued up Western. At Irving Park Road she turned west. "Where are we going?" I asked.

"I need a drink. You okay with that?"

"Sure," I said. "There's an Irish place just past the highway."

A few minutes later, we went under the highway. "How about Pelly's?" Susan said. "Is that still there?"

"Looks like." I pointed to the sign just ahead on the left. "You sure about this?" I asked as she turned into the parking lot.

"Oh, why not?" Susan said. "You're not afraid of ghosts, are you?"

Once upon a time Pelly's, a dark steakhouse with a cozy piano bar, had been our favorite spot. Our first visit had been one of those nights you always remember. After we married it became our special place. We'd gone there for just about every anniversary, every birthday, any romantic occasion.

But our last visit had been one of those nights you try hard to forget, and I hadn't been inside since.

We found a table in the furthest corner of the bar room. The piano bar was dark. But amber lights glowed, red candles twinkled here and there, while Tony Bennett sang softly.

"To what?" Susan held up her drink when it arrived.

"Laura," I said, and we clicked glasses and drank.

"So where were we?" Susan said. "What were we talking about?"

"Maybe Laura just left on her own."

"And your friend just happened to pick that day to die?"

"Stranger things have happened."

"Have you ever had an original thought?"

"I thought we were gonna be polite."

"Okay," she said. "Sorry. But maybe your friend tried something. I mean Laura's a good looking girl and he's a lonely old man."

"I don't see it."

"Laura fights back and your friend keels over. It wouldn't take much at his age. Agreed?"

"Yeah. Sure. But Ace wasn't that kind of guy."

"Middle of the night, all alone, guys get all sorts of strange notions."

"Okay. Let's say that's what happens," I said. "Ace makes some kind of pass. Laura fights back and Ace has a heart attack. So she gets scared and she gathers up all her stuff--this was several suitcases full--and then what? She can't carry it all."

"Come on. You're a cabdriver. What do you think?"

"So she takes a cab back to the Greyhound."

"Or the airport."

"Or the train," I said. "I don't see Ace trying anything. But maybe you're right. Maybe she just left."

"But why would she leave?" Susan said. "I thought you guys were having such a great time?"

"I might have exaggerated that," I said. "I mean, I was having a great time, It was like a dream come true. And I couldn't believe how cool she was. But she wasn't happy. She tried to pretend she was but she wasn't really. Every apartment we looked at she found something wrong with. She wouldn't even get out of the car to look at a single school. So, you know, thinking about it now, maybe she never planned to stay. Even the first night, she broke down in tears."

"Over what?"

"She said she was tired. The long trip and

100

everything."

"Something must have happened in California."

"What?"

"It's the only thing that makes sense," she said. "She wasn't running to Chicago. She was running away from California. Maybe they pulled something out there."

"What?"

"Don't know. I'm having a hard time imagining Scott getting anybody that pissed off. He was in the marching band and the jazz club. I mean, come on. But there he is, dead in the water."

"How about your husband?" I said.

"What about him?"

"Laura said something happened between them."

"What?"

"He did something to her," I said. "She told me it was more than just touching."

"Oh, bullshit! You just made that up."

"She said he was a creep."

"Oh, come on." She sat up straight and downed her drink. "Tell me what he did."

"I don't know."

"Well, didn't you ask her?"

"Of course I asked. She wouldn't say. She said he told her he might want to get together with her when she was older."

"Bullshit."

"Hook up, that's the term she used."

"If he said anything like that, which I seriously doubt, it was just Dan being Dan. He's an ex-cop. That's just weird cop humor."

"Yeah. Very funny."

"Dan loves Laura. I mean why would she go stay in his house if she thought he was a creep? That makes no sense."

"I'm just telling you what she said."

She signaled the waitress for another round. "What was she doing living with that old man, anyway? Why wasn't she staying with you?"

"She should have been," I said. I told her about Laura showing up at the Greyhound station and then ending up at Ace's while they searched for me. "If my phone hadn't been dead..."

"Yeah, sure," Susan said. "If a chicken had teeth."

"If we're gonna start accusing each other, why the hell would you go to Rio and leave an eighteen-year-old girl home alone?"

"I was out of the house at sixteen. Anyway, it was Laura's idea, a second honeymoon, getting back with Dan, being a family again. She really wanted that. I was pretty much ambivalent."

"Couldn't you have found her somewhere to stay?"

"Eddie, she's not a little kid. She's got her own car and a driver's license. She goes wherever she wants. She's got a boyfriend. She's been taking birth control pills since she was fifteen."

"Thanks for telling me that," I said.

"Oh, give me a break. You're remembering the little girl you used to know. I've got news for you. She's all grown up, or thinks she is. She doesn't listen to her mother, and she obviously didn't listen to you."

"I'm not the one who left her alone," I said.

"No. You left her with some old man who could

be a registered pedophile for all you know."

We went back and forth. We each scored a few points but we didn't get one inch closer to Laura.

"Look we both fucked up," Susan said after a while. "I didn't do a very good job of looking out for her at home. You didn't do a very good job of finding out why she came here."

"I thought we had all the time in the world."

"I was working so many hours," she said. "I picked up a second job."

"Again?"

"I don't like being poor, Eddie. You should know that. But she seemed happy. I swear to god. She loved Scott for some unknown reason. And, I don't care what you say, she liked Dan, too. They always had fun together."

"That's not what she told me."

A light came up over the piano and someone tinkled the keys. "Oh, my god," Susan said. "He's still here. He must be eighty-five."

"I see some old familiar faces out there," the piano player spoke into a microphone. "Let's see if I can remember..." And he started into a Tom Jones song we'd always requested.

"You believe this?" Susan said. She grabbed my hand and danced it along the table top for a few seconds. "Give me some money," she said when the song was almost done.

"What?"

"For his tip jar. I'm short on cash."

I fanned out my roll and she pulled a twenty from it. She walked up and dropped it into the tip jar then whispered in the piano player's ear.

"You're awful generous with other people's money," I said when she got back.

"You were always a sport, Eddie. You just never had enough."

After another round of drinks and a few more of our favorite songs, Susan's hand reached out under the table and found mine. "This okay?"

"Sure," I said.

"So tell me about all your girlfriends," she said after a while.

"I wish."

"Oh, come on. There has to be somebody."

"The girl next door was the longest," I said. "That lasted about four years."

"What happened to her?"

"She fell in love."

"So you got scared and chased her away."

"She didn't fall in love with me. Some old high school friend who found her on the internet. Last I heard they were happily married down in Kentucky."

"Well, at least someone's happy."

"Exactly what I told her."

We finished our drinks. I paid then we waved goodbye and walked out to the parking lot.

"You think you could escort me home?" Susan asked.

"To California?"

"To the Holiday Inn. We can have a nightcap at the bar."

"Sure. You want me to drive?"

"Absolutely not."

TWENTY-NINE

At the hotel we walked right past the bar. "Let me just change shoes," Susan said and I followed her up to her room.

She turned on the light and kicked off her shoes then reached up and undid her ear rings. "Can that drink wait until later?" she said.

I shrugged. "I'm okay without it."

"Could you do me a favor?" she asked.

"What?"

She brushed her hair away from her face. "Fuck me, Eddie. You think you could do that? For old times."

"Sure," I said. "Probably." But I wasn't convinced she was serious until she stripped down to bra and panties.

"You never had much finesse," she said a while later. "But you've still got the power. That was always your strong point."

"Is that a compliment?"

"You know I've been fantasizing about you for years," she said.

"Really?"

"Yeah," she said. "Right there. Strong and slow. Just. Like. That."

A while later, she woke me with a whisper. "You ever fantasize about me?"

"Way too much," I said.

"So tell me your favorite."

"Oh, come on. You know."

And she did. She remembered lick for lick.

"Just like the old days," she said a while later.

"Yeah. Cheating on your husband again."

"You still think I cheated on you?" she said.

"Hell, I know you did."

"Not once, Eddie. Not even after you turned into a piece of shit."

"What's the point of lying now?"

"Could you shut up and hold me?"

I held her tight for a while then we ended up on our backs staring at the ceiling.

"Do you remember the night we met?" Susan asked after a while.

"Sure," I said. "The Bitter End." This was a nightclub that had been just off the corner of Belmont and Central. "We should have figured it wasn't going to end well."

"You know I wasn't sure you weren't gay at first. You didn't even kiss me until the third date."

"Are you nuts? We spent half an hour in the phone booth that first night."

"Oh, that's right."

"And nobody called anybody gay back then."

"You sure took your sweet time about things. That's all I'm saying."

"I had an old girlfriend to deal with, remember?"

"Oh, yeah," she said. "Little Debbie."

"You never even met her," I said. "How can you be jealous of someone you don't know?"

"Aren't you jealous of Dan?"

"I'm jealous he got all those years with Laura," I said. "Why the hell did you have to meet someone in California, anyway?"

"I shouldn't have married him in the first place,"

she said. "It was just such an easy way out of Chicago--away from you, away from this fucking weather. I still don't understand why anyone lives here."

"So are you guys back together or what?"

"What," she said.

THIRTY

I awoke in the middle of the night and found Susan sitting up in bed. "You okay?" I asked.

"No," she said. "How about you?"

"I was thinking about who might have grabbed Laura."

"Join the club."

"Your husband."

"Get serious." She turned on the bedside lamp.

"Why not?"

"Why would he? And, anyway, he was with me in Rio and then he went to Florida."

"And he's a big-time drug dealer, right?"

"Is that what she said?"

"He doesn't work. He's always on the phone. He's always got money and he drives a brand new car."

"Oh, that little dimwit," she said.

"She said she found a big ball of drugs in the bathroom one day."

"Well, come on, everybody does a little," she said. "He's a movie producer for god's sake."

"Oh, give me a break."

"Seriously. L.A.'s full of 'em. Independent movie producers."

"Seems to me his daughter would know that. I mean, isn't that something you brag about?"

"Look, it's basically a con. He gets people to invest in movies that almost never get made."

"So what happens to the money?"

"Oh, it paid our mortgage for a while. Stuff like that."

"So Laura's right. He is a crook. Maybe he had a big bundle of cash and Scott and Laura grabbed it."

"There wasn't any bundle of cash," she said. "He doesn't have that kind of money. Believe me, I would know."

"I don't know," I said. "First Rio, then Florida. Sounds like money to me. And they're kids. A little bundle would probably do. And Laura did have money. I don't know how much. But she never asked me for a dime."

When I came out after a morning shower, Susan's suitcase was open on the bed. She was busy packing.

"Leaving so soon?"

"Yeah. Time to go home."

"California?"

"That's where I live."

"What about Dead-eye? We're supposed to see him at four."

She stopped her packing and gave me a level look. "He doesn't care and he's probably incompetent, anyway. But you know what? That's okay. Because if Laura and Scott did pull something in California, do we really want the Chicago Police Department knowing about it?"

"But who's gonna look for her?"

"Maybe she's already home. And if she's not,

maybe I can find out what she was up to while I was on vacation."

"I should come with you."

"I don't have room for you, Eddie."

"They've got hotels out there."

"Eddie, let me get home first and see what's going on. One way or the other, I need to have a nice long talk with Dan."

"I wouldn't mind being in on that."

"No. You want to stay as far away as possible. He's not a cop anymore. But he still thinks he is."

"There's nothing stopping us going to the real police out there."

"No. No. No," she said. "Most cops are fuck-ups. Believe me. I know that now. Let me try to find out what's going on. Then if we have to, we call 'em."

"I'm coming with you," I said.

"No. You're not," she said, and there was no arguing with that voice.

"Fuck," I said. "You know, I'm still not sure you didn't take her."

"Yes you are," she said. "You know I didn't fly two thousand miles just to throw you a fuck."

"Yeah. I guess you're right." And there I was, getting yanked by her chain once again. Still pussy-whipped after all these years.

"It was nice," she said.

"What?"

"Come on. Wasn't it?"

"Sure. Just like old times," I said.

"Better," she said. "Look, I'll call you every day. Promise. Okay?"

She dropped me off on Lawrence Avenue just

before the highway. "What do I tell Dead-eye?" I asked, standing outside the driver's window.

"Don't tell him anything. Don't talk to him at all. Don't talk to your sergeant either. Just leave well enough alone."

I watched as the car moved down the entrance ramp. "Well enough?" I shouted after it. "There's nothing well enough about any of this."

A horn sounded behind me. I turned around to find myself standing in the middle of the street. I'd been talking to myself, too.

THIRTY-ONE

I took the bus home, sat down at the kitchen table, got up, put the kettle on, and the next thing I knew the pot was whistling and I still didn't have a thought in my head.

I wasn't supposed to talk to Dead-eye or the sergeant. Maybe Susan was right: What the police didn't know wouldn't hurt them. But even if she wasn't, I'd go along. Because I always had. She'd always been smarter. Always the go-getter. I'd long suspected that one of the reasons she'd agreed to marry me was because I'd been so good at following orders. Why would I change now?

I made my tea then watched it cool.

I dug through my wallet and found the card the sergeant had given me: Michael Cantore Investigations.

"Fuck her," I said to the walls. And I realized my favorite part of Susan's visit was when she'd apologized after I'd gotten out of her car and walked away.

110

I should have done that years ago. But I'd been too afraid of losing Laura, losing Susan, living on my own. But I'd lost them both, anyway, and ended up alone. And I'd lost a load of self-respect in the process.

I didn't trust her. It was that simple. I never had. "You know I didn't come two thousand miles just to throw you a fuck," she'd said. And that was certainly true. But that didn't mean I knew why she'd come.

Maybe she was telling the truth. She'd come home from Rio and found Laura gone. Maybe she'd never been to Rio. Maybe the only vacation she'd taken was to Chicago to drag Laura back home or to some Utah re-education camp. Yeah. She had a beautiful sun tan but that you could get at any mall in America.

Even back in our happily married days, I'd never really trusted her. She had the habit of disappearing for long hours and then coming home with the flimsiest of excuses. Once she'd come back with a sly smile and told me she'd been flipping through magazines at Walgreen's and had lost track of the time.

"Flipping through magazines for four hours?"

"Here. I brought you one." She handed me a woman's magazine. On the cover a headline read: FIFTY WAYS TO TELL IF YOUR SPOUSE IS CHEATING. "Look at number one," she said.

I turned to an inside page. *Number one: Does your spouse seem a lot happier lately?*

"That's not us, right?" she'd said.

THIRTY-TWO

"Pardon the outfit," Mike Cantore said as he led me into his one-room office. "I spent half the day in a courtroom." He was a big guy with a beard, a mustache, and a head of bushy hair, all in various shades of grey. He took off his suit jacket, hung it on a hook then loosened his tie. "Make yourself comfortable," he said, and he moved behind the desk and pretty much disappeared.

The office was out along Harlem Avenue, two miles south of the highway to O'Hare. This was as close as you could get to the suburbs without really being there. It was on the second floor above a real-estate office and down the hall from a small law firm.

There was a large window at the back of the room. But the blinds were down and only a bit of daylight got through. The only other light was from a desk lamp which the detective hid behind.

He pushed a small recorder to the middle of the desk top. "Do you mind if I record this for my files?" I shook my head. "This is a recording of a conversation between Eddie Miles and Michael Cantore, made with the consent of both parties."

As I told my story, the detective took an occasional note and twirled his pen. "Well, I hate to say it," he said when I was done. "But I think you're right not to rely on the police. It's a new regime. In the old days they wanted as much crime as they could find to justify their budget. Now they want as little as possible so they can justify the cuts they're making. Funny world, huh?"

I agreed that it was a funny world. *A private eye.*

Cantore was the first one I'd met outside of books. He was about as exciting as your typical insurance agent.

"Okay. It seems to me that the two people who we'd really like to know about here are your ex and her new hubby. And let's add the boyfriend, too. Scott no last name."

"I could call the ex."

"If he died off Malibu, that shouldn't be too hard to find. And the new hubby's an ex-cop. I shouldn't have any trouble getting a line on him. Cops love to talk. And once they start it's like opening a faucet. Now you probably don't have your ex's driver's license number, credit card numbers, anything like that?"

I shook my head. "Sorry."

"Do you know if she used a credit card while she was here?"

"She bought lunch with one. The Alps, Irving and Lincoln."

"A diner, right?"

"One of the few things she misses about Chicago."

"Good. Now this rent-a-car. Hertz? Avis? Dollar?"

"Don't know."

"License plate?"

"No."

"She run any red lights where the camera might have gotten her or did she get pulled over for speeding, anything like that?"

"Not while I was along."

"You're sure she flew in at O'Hare?"

"That's what she said."

"Airline?"

"Sorry."

"Don't worry," he said. "We've got a little to work with and that's usually all you need to get started. Now the problem is, it's gonna take time. A couple of days at least to really get anywhere and time is money. So it's gonna cost."

"How much?"

"It's usually a hundred and twenty-five an hour."

"Whoa!"

He held up his hands, palms out. "But you being a cabdriver and all I think we could bring that down to seventy five. What do you say?"

"How about fifty?"

"Deal." He stood up and leaned across the desk to give me a handshake. "First I'll need a retainer of oh, let's say five hundred and then just forget about it for twenty-four hours. Hibernate. Don't call me unless you have something new. If you don't hear from me by tomorrow night, feel free to call. I might have something by then."

THIRTY-THREE

That night, I stopped only for people who waved correctly, their arm up and out from their body, their head facing the cab. I wasn't stopping for index fingers, nods of the head, or side-straddle hops. Raising the hem of a skirt got you nowhere, especially if you were a guy. Whistling didn't do it either, unless you happened to be a doorman.

People with the correct flagging technique got into my cab and eventually got out and hardly a word was spoken. I was lost in my own world with a missing daughter, a dead friend, and an ex-wife I suddenly couldn't stop thinking about.

I hadn't had a steady woman in years and I'd pretty much given up looking. I'd told myself that I was too old, too fat, and too ornery. I'd gone so long without a woman that I'd all but forgotten what to do. But then Susan had shown up and it turned out the old saying was true. It was just like riding a bike. It had all come back and I wanted more.

"Turn left," the drunk in the back seat said. It was after midnight and, as usual, half the city was in the bag. This one had been staggering just off Rush Street. But, drunk as he was, he'd still managed to flag me properly.

"Why?" I continued heading south on State.

"Hey, go back. Take me through the McDonald's."

"Sorry, buddy. I don't do drive-thru's."

"I'll buy you a hamburger."

"Thanks but no thanks."

"Hey, dude, what's your fucking problem? I'm paying you."

"Not anymore you're not." I flicked the meter off, pulled to the side and stopped. "I think I can live without your five dollars."

A few minutes later, I was sitting at a red light on Chicago Avenue when a young black guy walked up to my window. "I just missed my bus," he said. "Can you take me to Central and Chicago?"

"Sure," I said. He opened the left door and got in behind me. In the days before bulletproof shields it was often a bad sign when someone wanted to sit directly behind the driver. But it really didn't matter anymore. He was sober. He looked like any other working man heading home.

115

I started west and went straight back to thinking about Susan.

For years she'd been the personification of the devil to me. I wasn't completely blind to my own problems. After losing my job, I'd been wallowing in booze and self-pity. But Susan hadn't shown an ounce of sympathy or compassion. She'd thrown me out at the lowest point of my life, and then had pushed me even lower by taking my daughter and moving her two thousand miles away.

Now she'd let me share her bed again, if only briefly. I didn't trust her motives. But that didn't stop me from wanting more. And it didn't stop the old memories. The ones I thought were gone.

"There's my bus," the guy in back said.

We'd caught up to the bus at California Avenue. The last of the white passengers were getting off. I looked in the mirror. "You want to get on it?"

"No," he said, still slouched over in the corner of the seat. "I'm in the cab."

We continued west, and I went back to my thoughts. One day I was holding Laura, who couldn't have been more than three, while Susan searched through her purse for parking meter change. Laura was singing a song with no words. The sun was streaking through Susan's blond hair, she was smiling, and I remember thinking, I'll never forget how beautiful she looks right now. *How beautiful they both looked that day. My family.* But I had forgotten until now.

We went under a viaduct and now we were officially in the ghetto. We passed Homan Avenue. Up ahead was the drug strip I'd shown Laura the

116

other night, with its flashing blue police cameras. I glanced back in the mirror and my passenger was now sitting dead center behind the opening in the shield, and suddenly he didn't look like a working man at all. The whites of his eyes were almost as dark as his skin. He was looking straight into the mirror, straight into my eyes.

"Nothing personal," I said when we stopped for the light at Pulaski. I reached back and closed the shield in his face.

"Oh, man, what the fuck?"

"Sorry, buddy. It's just this fucking neighborhood."

"No. It's just 'cause I'm black. Ain't that the truth?"

"You can think whatever you want," I said.

"I think you're a racist pig." He went on in that way for a while and I stopped listening. But I wasn't thinking about Susan either. I was looking forward to the moment he was out of the cab.

I glanced in the mirror as we passed Cicero Avenue. He'd moved back to the corner of the seat. I stopped for the red light at Laramie, a half mile from Central Avenue, and the left door opened. "Fuck you, man," he said as he ran away.

I heard the distinctive horn of a squad car. I turned my head and found two young and eager-looking cops parked in the gas station off to the right. One of them pointed the way the guy had gone then lifted his hand in question. I shrugged and waved: *Don't bother*. They waved back. It was just another night in the ghetto.

———

THIRTY-FOUR

I turned left, heading for the highway back to the Loop, but when I got to Madison Street, I turned west instead.

I'd skipped Austin when Laura and I had taken our tour of the city's worst neighborhoods. For some reason Austin still broke my heart. It was one of the few places where I could still feel the old city, the city of my youth.

I found myself having a silent, one-sided, conversation, telling Laura about the old days on the West Side back when Madison was a thriving commercial street. We'd moved from Lincoln Park when I was a kid, fleeing the Puerto Ricans and white trash then moving in. We'd arrived in Austin just a few years before the West Side exploded in rage.

It was a great looking neighborhood at first. It even smelled better than Lincoln Park. The houses were further apart. The air was cleaner. There were plenty of trees and lots of grass on the side streets. Columbus Park, right across Adams Boulevard from our new home, had playgrounds and baseball diamonds, waterfalls with flagstone steps, a nine-hole golf course, a swimming pool, and a large lagoon where a recorded message would play on late into spring: "Danger. Thin ice. Keep Off. No skating." Over and over it broadcast the same message, usually long after the ice had melted. But for some reason it was no more irritating than the bagpipers who practiced in the park all summer long.

I didn't know anyone out this way at first. In

memory, I spent the entire summer going to the movies. The State Theater was on Madison Street just a block from my house. The Madison bus would take me east to the Bird, the Marbro, and the Alex.

Sometimes if I was bored, or if I'd already seen all the movies, I would take the bus all the way downtown. This took me through the black neighborhood which back then bordered Garfield Park.

A few years later this was the center of the riot zone and most of the whites in Austin decided that was too close for comfort. They moved out and the blacks--burned out of their old neighborhoods by the riots--moved in. "How could they mess up such a beautiful place?" my father had muttered in suburban exile until the day he'd died. "They" were sometimes the new black residents, sometimes panic-peddling real-estate agents, sometimes the FHA offering virtually-no-money-down loans, sometimes our white neighbors who had fled in droves over a single summer. Whoever you wanted to blame, within a couple of years, this section of Austin was part of the black West Side.

But in those early years Austin was a great place. Madison Street was a teeming, bustling, slow-moving commercial street. A window seat on the Madison bus offered a great view for a kid with no friends.

September came and I went to school. I made a few friends and then a few more with the boys who hung on the corner on Madison, and before too long I had an after school job, my first car, and even a real girlfriend.

I drove south to Jackson Boulevard and followed along as it curved gently through the park. I went by the old homestead--a vast six-flat that would have been worth millions in Lincoln Park--and turned down the narrow side street where one night we'd strolled as the noise of a party receded in the background. We'd stopped in the shadow of a towering elm and soon the only sound was our breathing. I went a few blocks over and past a different house where in the middle of the night the same girl had whispered, "Was it your first time?"

Yeah. It was. And we were both younger than Laura at the time. So, of course, Susan was right. Laura wasn't a little girl anymore. Were she and Scott lovers? That was something I preferred not to think about. I wondered when the detective would get around to calling. What would he find?

I stopped briefly but our tree was long gone. The elms and their lush canopy had disappeared even before the neighborhood, the victims of Dutch elm disease.

A cul-de-sac cut off the block from Madison Street. I turned around quickly before any of the current corner boys got any ideas. I wondered if they were really any more criminal than we'd been.

When people had complained that the cul-de-sacs actually made the neighborhoods more dangerous, the mayor said, "You can't have a drive-by shooting if people can't drive by." That got a big laugh when Tony Golden read it aloud at the roundtable one night.

The bench was still there in the back corner of the playground--where we sat and kissed and planned

120

for a future that was nothing but a dream. I wondered if that old Park District slogan was still branded in the wood: No Petting or Necking. It certainly hadn't stopped us.

Up on Madison Street, if I squinted a bit, I could see the ever moving line where the shadow met the sun while we played game after game of fast pitching. All we needed was a ball, a bat, and a batters' box painted on a brick wall. I could almost hear the sound the rubber ball made as it hit the bricks and bounced from shade back into sunshine.

The brick wall was long gone. Across the street, the State Theater was gone, too. But I remembered the old marquee and then the new one, which had come from the Congress Theater, not too far from our old Lincoln Park home.

Moving from Lincoln Park to Austin had seemed like a good idea at one time. But it quickly became the family joke, a joke that was never uttered anywhere near my father. Lincoln Park had been on the skids back then, a lower middle class neighborhood that appeared to be headed straight down. Now the old Lincoln Park block was dotted with huge million dollar houses, with new ones sprouting every day, even in the midst of a housing crisis.

The only thing sprouting in Austin were empty lots, as scores of beautiful old buildings returned to dust. But through that haze I could still glimpse the faded outline of the old city. In Lincoln Park--where I cruised night after night in my cab--it was impossible to see the old days. The sparkle of money had obliterated all signs of the past. Only the glittering future mattered.

Lincoln Park was part of the new city, the city where Tony Golden's conspiracy theory came true, the city of the rich. Austin still held memories for me. But it was truly the city of the poor now, the city of the left-behinds, the city of failure. Maybe that's why I felt so at home.

I'd failed at school, at work, with my family. And when I'd been given a second chance I'd failed once again. Was Laura gone forever? Was this to be my final failure?

I'd lost her once because of money and I'd sworn that that would never happen again. I'd saved every penny I could, worked day after day, so I'd be ready if she arrived. I'd buy her a car or a college education. I'd help her out with a down payment on a small condo and pay for her wedding. I'd do all the things that any good father would. I wouldn't be a deadbeat the second time around.

I'd waited all those years, never leaving Chicago, never changing apartments or my phone, dreaming of the day she'd return. Now she was gone and if my worst fears came true then Chicago would truly be the city of the past for me, with nothing but bad memories.

I was almost downtown cruising through what had once been Skid Row, when a couple waved from in front of one of the new sports bars.

When I stopped, the guy motioned for me to make a U-turn. I stayed right where I was on the other side of the street. This was also from Ace's rule book. Illegal U-turns were usually unnecessary and should never be made if you were the only cab in sight. After a bit of hesitation, the couple walked across.

The guy opened the door, gave the girl a hug, then closed it behind her.

"Armitage and Clark," she said.

I was pointed in the exact right direction. "So why was I supposed to make a U-turn," I said as I started away. She began weeping.

"Lady, in ten years you won't even remember his name," I said. This was my standard line for crying girls.

"No. No," she said. "It's not a boy."

"Sorry."

"Thank you for trying to make me feel better. I wish it were a boy."

"Oh."

"My brother died."

"I'm sorry," I said.

"It's been almost six months," she said. "But I was with a whole group of his friends tonight and it brings it all back."

"Sure."

"I don't think I'll ever get over it."

"With time," I said.

"But I don't want to get over it, don't you see? I want to keep his memory close. I don't want to forget."

THIRTY-FIVE

Mike Cantore finally called.

"Well, your daughter didn't leave the driving to Greyhound, at least not under her own name. But that doesn't mean she didn't take the train or fly. But

I don't have those connections. Here's the big thing. Looks like the new hubby is a definite kink."

"You found him?"

"Pretty sure. Dan Payne." He spelled it out for me. "He's got a wife named Susan and a daughter named Laura. He got tossed off the force in Bay City. A woman said he offered to let her off on a traffic ticket if she'd appear in a movie he was making."

"So maybe he really is a movie producer," I said, and I remembered that he'd met Susan when he pulled her over for speeding.

"She auditioned for him, which meant taking off her clothes but then he wanted a blow job. After that made the news, all these other women came forward, 'Oh, yeah, he tried that with me, too.' One girl was just disappointed that she didn't get to be in the movie. 'It was just a blow job,' she said. 'It wasn't like we had sex or anything.'

"Anyway, they never did charge him but they forced him to resign. So that was the end of his public service. He's been buying and selling foreclosures. Looks like he's got an in with one of the bankers. So he buys 'em and then flips 'em to some remodelers who can't deal with the banks. But nobody thinks there's much money in that, and he's been living large. He bought himself a new house and a Mercedes. The going theory is that he's dealing or transporting drugs. He owns a piece of a boat. Him and eight other guys, cops or ex-cops. So he only gets it so many days a year. But it's got a good size hold so how many trips do you need?

"I couldn't find much on the movie producer

124

angle. Some think it's a con like your ex says, or maybe just a way to get the occasional blow job. There're rumors that he's producing porno films in the foreclosed houses. He's using them as sets in some series called 'Fuck This House/Fuck the Bank.' The actors go around having sex room to room while they're trashing the place. But, once again, that's just a rumor. We had a lot of fun looking for the finished product but we never found it. So the general consensus is that he's a drug dealer or maybe just a trafficker."

"Which is what Laura said."

"Right. And they did go to Rio for Carnival. It's not cheap, either. So that gave your daughter and her boyfriend plenty of time to search the house. So maybe they did mess with his money."

"Or with his drugs," I said.

"Here's the funny thing. They've got a pocket full of credit cards. And they both use theirs all the time. Especially your ex. But he's barely used his since he got back from Rio."

"He's on a fishing trip," I said.

"Okay. That explains that. He's out on the boat. So maybe he's bringing in another load."

"No. She says he went to Florida. The gulf coast, I think, some fish he's always wanted to catch."

"So how come I'm not finding any tickets to Florida on his charge card."

"Maybe he drove," I said.

"That's a long drive to go fishing, especially if you've got your own boat. But same question. How come I'm not finding charges for gas and motels?"

"Well, if he really is a drug dealer wouldn't he

have a lot of cash to get rid of?"

"Yeah, maybe," Cantore said, "if the kids didn't snag it. But let's say he didn't go to Florida. He came up here instead and the reason he didn't use his credit card, he didn't want anybody to know it."

"So how do we find out?"

"I'm trying to get a driver's license number for him or a plate number so I can search for tickets he might have gotten along the way. But if he didn't get any tickets or didn't use his own car, that's gonna be a dead end. Let me ask you this: Did you ever spot anyone could have been watching your apartment or Ace's house?"

"No."

"Ever get the feeling you were being followed. Same car behind you all the time or a car running a red light to keep up with you."

"No," I said. "Wait. There was a car that ran a red light and got the camera flashing."

"When was this?"

"Laura was with me. I think it was the last night. We were going north on Western and a guy behind us in a minivan ran the light at Peterson. I wouldn't have noticed except the camera went off. And of course, he got the next light, anyway. So what did he save for his ninety dollar contribution to the city?"

"So what day is this? What time?"

"Midnight or later."

"This might be the break we need. But remember when I was telling you about expenses. This is gonna be one of 'em, for me to get a look at that film."

"How much?"

"A hundred, at least. Maybe as much as five. Depends who's working."

"That's a lot of money," I said. "I mean, what are the odds?"

"You want to find your daughter or not?"

THIRTY-SIX

Mike Cantore called again later that night. "That was a pickup truck that ran that light the other night," he said.

"I thought it was a minivan."

"No. Ford pickup with a camper top," he said. "California plates."

"You're kidding?"

"No. But unfortunately it's registered to one Reginald R. Reilly."

"So a waste of money, right?"

"Well, maybe it's just a coincidence. I mean there're millions of cars with California plates. But not that many make it up here, especially in the middle of winter. I've got a fuzzy picture of the driver. You don't happen to know what the new hubby looks like."

"Sorry."

"Well, no worry. I'm gonna e-mail it out there, have someone who knows him take a look, just on the off chance that he borrowed this Reilly's truck."

"Maybe I'll go out there myself," I said.

"California?"

"Yeah," I said. "Why not? And this gives me a good excuse. Can you make me a copy of that picture?"

"Sure. You're not thinking of doing anything crazy, are you?"

"I'm trying to find my daughter. Isn't that the point?"

The other point: I was going crazy doing nothing in Chicago.

THIRTY-SEVEN

I dialed Susan's number over and over and listened to her recorded message. *I'll call you every day*, she'd promised me. So far I hadn't heard a word.

"I thought you were gonna call me," I said when she finally answered.

"As soon as I know something," she said.

"Laura's not there, I take it."

"No Laura and no Dan. He's supposed to be back from Florida but I can't find him."

"Interesting. Hey, there's a picture I'd like you to take a look at."

"Of what?"

"Somebody running a red light behind me and Laura."

"What am I looking for?"

"See if you recognize anyone?"

"What are the odds of that?"

"California license plates."

"Really?"

"Really."

"What kind of car?"

"A Ford pickup truck."

"Hmm. Nobody I know."

"I thought I might bring the picture out."

"You ever hear of the computer age?"

"I'd kind of like to talk to Laura's friends, too."

"Look, work's a mess. I'm trying to get a divorce and trying to track down Laura and Dan. I don't have time for you right now, Eddie. Give me another couple days, okay?"

"Sure," I said, agreeable as always. She gave me an e-mail address and I wrote it down.

"How'd you find this picture?" she asked.

"A detective."

"Dead-eye?"

"No. A private guy."

"How'd he find you?"

"I hired him."

"You hired a private detective?"

"Right."

"Do you really want our dirty laundry all over the street?"

"It's not my dirty laundry," I said, and the phone went dead in my ear.

THIRTY-EIGHT

Paki Bob was the star of the roundtable that night. He was actually a Berber from Algiers. He'd come to Chicago years ago to go to graduate school. But he'd gotten sidetracked into the cab business and had never gotten out.

Way back when, his fellow cabdrivers had mistaken him for a Pakistani and he'd been too timid to correct them. He was timid no more. He was now officially rich.

He'd managed to accumulate five taxi medallions when prices were low, which he'd leased out to fellow Berbers. He'd just sold four of them for a total of $1.2 million.

"Bet you don't hate America so much anymore?" Ken Willis said.

"I never hated America," Paki said. "I love America. It's Americans I can't stand."

"You son of a bitch!"

"You sit in here all night drinking coffee complaining that you can't make any money. Go out and work. Then you'll make money."

"There's no money out there this time of night," Fat Wally said.

"There's always money," Paki said. "Right, Eddie?"

"Yeah," I said. "You just gotta go find it."

And you had to pretty much give up your life. And that's what I'd done, day after day for years. It was the rare night when I didn't get behind the wheel. No vacations. No weekends off. No nights on the town. No woman to worry about. No kids to support. But you needed the energy. And I didn't have it anymore. I was like the rest of the losers now.

"And how many of you won medallions in the lottery?" Paki shouted. "And you sold them for peanuts so you could throw the money away on horses."

Escrow Jake looked out the window as if no one were talking about him.

"Hey, Bob, what are you gonna do with all that money?"

"My name is not Bob," he said for about the millionth time. "My name is Said."

"Now that you've got all that money, maybe we'll

call you the Berber King."

"Maybe I'll buy this place and throw you out to the street."

"I'm thinking of going to California tomorrow," I said to Ken Willis.

"Does that mean she's out there?"

"No. Not according to the ex. But I want to see for myself."

"Who you flying?"

"I figured I'd just go out to O'Hare, see who's got a seat."

"Are you nuts? That'll cost you a fortune."

His loud voice got everyone's attention and the next thing I knew my trip was the center of attention. Everybody agreed I couldn't just go to the airport. Fat Wally went out to his cab and came back with his computer. It didn't take long to find me a round-trip ticket for three hundred dollars. But I suddenly got cold feet. Was I really going? "I'll call you when I know for sure," I said.

"When's the last time you were out of town?" Ken Willis asked.

"I had a trip to Kenosha a couple of months back."

"Come on," Ken said. "A real trip?"

"We took Laura to Disney World when she was six."

"You haven't been out of Chicago in twelve years?" This seemed to amaze Ken.

"Hell," Fat Wally said, "I haven't been out of town since '86, which is when I lost seven grand in Vegas. I wish I'd never gone that time either."

"Hey, did you ever renew your chauffeur's license?" Ken asked. This was something we usually did together. But this year, with Laura around, Ken had gone without me.

"I've still got until the end of the month," I said.

"Better do it before you go," Ken said. "Who knows how long you'll be out there. Remember what happened to Phil Milano."

Milano was a high school English teacher who'd driven a cab every summer for years. One summer he went to Europe instead. He didn't bother to renew his license that year and when he tried to do it the next year, the city told him that since he'd let his license lapse for more than a month he'd have to take the same two week course that all new drivers were now forced to attend. Milano refused. He was a teacher and a poet. Not a student. Now many summer nights, he came by the roundtable to bitch and moan.

"I'll do it tomorrow," I said, and then said goodbye.

I cruised around for a while ferrying the drunks home. And then I called the day driver from the gas station to tell him I was quitting early.

"Owner is selling cab," he said with a heavy accent.

"What?"

"He is selling medallion today. He said he would call you."

"Shit," I said. "What do I do with the car?"

"Not my problem," he said, sounding like a true American. "I'm back asleep."

The phone rang as the gas pump clicked off.

"Ernie," I said into it. "You said you were never gonna sell."

"Three hundred and twenty thousand dollars." he said. "You come over here and explain to my wife why she's got to keep working."

"Hey, no big deal," I said. "I was gonna take a little vacation, anyway."

"Leave it in the usual spot on Western. Put the keys in the ashtray. Oh, and don't bother gassing up."

"Too late, I just did."

"Oh, well, I should have called you earlier. I meant to."

"I'll see you around."

"Yeah. Take care, Eddie. Maybe I'll stop by that pancake house some night."

I double-parked in front of my apartment and dropped a flash light, various tools and pads of cab receipts, and a pair of sunglasses into my cab bag, then grabbed a taxi guide, a street guide, and a six-county atlas from the door panels.

I popped the trunk and pulled out a milk crate. Inside were two quarts of oil, transmission fluid, a can of WD-40, a bottle of Windex, and a roll of paper towels. I left behind an umbrella and several mismatched gloves.

For years, I'd been transferring the milk crate from cab to cab. I couldn't remember the last time I'd actually been without a taxi. When I got back from California I'd start looking for another.

THIRTY-NINE

I liked riding buses. I always saw plenty that I missed while driving the same streets in the cab. I even liked waiting at bus stops if it wasn't too cold.

It usually reminded me of my days as a juvenile delinquent, hanging out with the corner boys on Madison Street watching the world go by.

But it felt strange not to have a car to call my own. Ernie's cab might not have been exclusively mine. But it had been mine from six at night until six in the morning seven nights a week, and that was usually all the wheels I needed.

Now I didn't have anything but the Chicago Transit Authority. The Montrose bus got me up to Western Avenue. But there wasn't a Western bus in sight.

Lack of wheels had gotten me into the cab business in the first place. I was recently divorced and delivering pizzas which was nice because it meant daily pay. Unfortunately, I was spending most of what I made just as quickly in one saloon or another.

I'd blown a head gasket on my Chevy but I didn't have enough money to fix it. Without the car, I was suddenly out of work. Someone in a bar suggested driving a cab to get the money for repairs.

This was the desperation job of choice back then. A few million Chicagoans before me had probably said, "Worse come to worse, I can always drive a cab."

The ad in the Tribune said, "A thinking fellow drives a Yellow." And that's where I went. They took what little money I had, gave me a two hour training course, and sent me downtown to take a twenty-five question test and be fingerprinted. Later that same day I had my temporary license and exclusive use of a shiny Yellow Cab.

And I actually liked the job. I'd always liked driving, and now I found that I didn't mind driving and driving and driving. I'd stop home to take a quick nap and count my money. I didn't have to wait for somebody to order a pizza. I could go out and find someone who needed a ride. I didn't have a boss breathing down my neck. Even the worst passengers were usually out of the cab in a couple of minutes.

Times had changed. Now, if you were starting out, you needed to go to a city school full time for two weeks. That cost a couple hundred bucks. After school, you had to take an 80-question test. If you passed that, you still had to take a drug test and a physical and pay for both out of your own pocket. The English proficiency test and fingerprints were free. But before you got your Chicago taxi license, got behind the wheel, and picked up your first passenger, you'd probably spend more than five hundred bucks and at least a month of your time. This was the main reason Americans no longer drove taxis. With their language problems, the foreign guys didn't have much choice. In what other job could they work every waking hour and support not only themselves but their families across the sea?

A bus finally came along. I took it seven miles south then walked around the corner to the city's office of Consumer Services. I was about to walk in the door when my phone rang.

"I found the boyfriend," Cantore said. "Scott Brasher. He washed up at Topanga Beach last week. He was in the water awhile and something got to him, a shark or a boat, so the body's a mess. No cause of death yet. They're waiting for toxicology reports. But that probably won't tell 'em if he drowned or not.

"Now here's the funny thing," he went on. "He got pulled over for an illegal U-turn on the 20th."

"What's so funny about that?"

"He was driving your daughter's car."

"Was she there?" This was three days before she showed up in Chicago.

"Don't know," he said. "But they ended up locking Scott up for failure to appear on a previous ticket, which meant he was driving on a suspended license. They wrote him for that and the U-turn and towed the car. He made bail the same day but the car wasn't released until the 25th."

"So how does this get us any closer to Laura?"

"Once again, don't know. The problem is there's no way of telling what's important until later. So you gotta go the long way around. I've got Scott's address. I thought if you ever do get to California you might want to talk to his family. See what they know."

"Sure," I said, and I wrote down an address in Van Nuys. "But it won't be until at least tomorrow. I've got to renew my chauffeur's license."

"It's always something, isn't it?"

"Hey, did you send that picture to my ex?" I asked.

"Yeah," he said. "I got an answer, too."

"What'd she say?"

"'It looks a bit like Eddie Miles.' That's a direct quote."

"Does it?"

"Well, a little, I guess. The guy's wearing a baseball cap so you don't really get that good of a view."

"We spent two hundred and we can't tell who it is?"

It was the usual mob scene inside the office. This is where every cabdriver in town came to renew his taxi license. If you were flying 747's around the planet your pilot's license didn't expire until you did. But a Chicago cabdriver's license expired every 12 months, and if you didn't renew it in a timely manner they'd tell you to fork over a couple of hundred bucks and waste two weeks going to school.

I handed in my driver's and my taxi license along with an abstract of my driving record, and waited while the receptionist filled out a sheet which she attached to a clipboard.

I scanned it. "Oh, give me a break," I said. "I took a continuing education course last year." This meant I couldn't get my license renewed until tomorrow at the earliest. I'd already missed today's class.

"If you have a ticket within the last two years you must take the course," she said.

"That doesn't make any sense. I took it the year before, too."

"I don't make the rules," she said.

I took a look at my driving record. I'd gotten caught speeding on Lake Shore Drive on March 14th, two years ago next week.

"Wait a minute," I said. "If the ticket's more than two years old I don't have to take the course?"

"That is correct."

"So if I wait until after the 14th, I don't have to take it?"

She grabbed my paperwork and looked at it, then took a long look at her desktop calendar. Then she gave me her definitive answer. "Maybe."

"That's the best you can do?"

"I don't want you coming back telling me I made you any promises."

Of course, if I waited until next week, my trip to California would be that much farther away. "Oh, what the hell," I said. "How bad can it be?"

I went down the street to the medical center paid $85 and pissed in a cup, then had my blood pressure tested and my heart listened to by a doctor who looked a bit like Boris Karloff.

Heading home on the Western Avenue bus, I tried Susan's number. "What's up?" I said when she answered, and pulled the exit cord. "Any news?"

"No. Not on this end. How about your detective, what did he find?"

"Hold on a second. I'm getting off the bus."

I got off in the industrial area north of Lake Street and walked along and told her about Cantore's progress to date. She seemed particularly interested in Scott's U-turn ticket.

"Your hubby home yet?"

"My soon-to-be ex is no longer answering his phone," she said.

"I know just how you feel," I said.

"I have to admit, it's got me wondering. I mean, maybe you're right. It doesn't make any sense. But none of this does."

138

"How about Reginald Reilly," I said. "That sound familiar?"

"No. Who is it?"

"That's the registration on that pick up truck. Reggie Reilly?"

"Nobody I know." She asked for Cantore's number and I couldn't see any reason not to give it to her. "Maybe you should come out here," she said.

"As soon as I can get my stupid hack license renewed."

FORTY

The continuing education class was scheduled to start at nine o'clock sharp. When I showed up at five to, there were three other drivers in the room. Several tables were laid out with sign-up sheets, pencils, and enough chairs for a couple of dozen. I picked a seat at the back table and waited as the room slowly filled.

The teacher came in with doughnuts and went around the room getting names. He was another American, a black guy somewhere around my age. But he didn't look familiar. I decided he must be a day driver, or maybe a front-office worker, in other words, a guy who had never actually driven a cab.

"What do you want to be called?" he asked everyone.

"Eddie," I said.

"You the Miles from that thing a few years back?" he asked.

I nodded. "Probably."

He gave me a long look. "Nice to meet you," he said.

A thin black guy sat next to me. "Same bullshit every year," he said with an accent.

"Help yourself to a doughnut," the teacher said. "If you brought coffee go ahead and drink it. If you brought alcoholic beverages, you've got to share."

Hotel Steve walked in. I caught his eye and nodded. He nodded back. This was the longest conversation we'd had in years.

"Okay, let's get down to business," the teacher said at nine-thirty. "Rule number one: A blow job is not an acceptable form of payment."

This brought the class to life. Shouts of "Why not?" "Sure it is." "What if it's their idea?"

"It doesn't make any difference whose idea it is," the teacher said. "You're taking advantage of an intoxicated girl. You're gonna lose your job and you might end up going to jail. It's not right. It's not worth it. Don't do it. End of discussion."

"Oh, man," the guy next to me said. "That's gonna put me out of business."

"You're here today because citizens are not happy," the teacher said. "The image they have of cabdrivers is pretty awful. Customers want comfort not speed. You're in the service business. Some drivers will curl your hair and those are the people the public remembers."

Like any bad class there were a couple of videos. The first was of an overly courteous cabdriver, driving from hotel to hotel somewhere in Florida. The lesson to be learned: You must earn your tips.

The next was from a local news station, an expose about cabdrivers talking on their cell phones. The camera ambushed a driver as he went around a corner with a phone attached to his ear. "Why do you have that phone?" an off-camera voice asked.

"It's permanently there," the driver said. This brought a roar from the class. The video was followed by a class discussion about cell phones and driving.

"The cops are all on the phone," one of the drivers said, "truck drivers, all these other mopes. Why can't we be on the phone?"

"Because we don't have power," the teacher said. "We don't have clout. Now I don't want to be giving away trade secrets here. But if you get off the phone and talk to your passengers you might make more money."

A small, bald guy jumped to his feet. "Is other way," he shouted.

"What other way?" the teacher asked.

"It's different for us," the driver said. "You are American."

"So what?" the teacher said.

"When I talk to my passengers there are many misunderstandings," the driver said. "I don't always understand what the passenger is saying. They don't understand what I am saying. This leads to nothing but trouble. It is better to say nothing, look straight ahead, and keep the phone to your ear."

"I can't argue with your logic," the teacher said.

My phone vibrated. It was Cantore. I got up and walked out and into the washroom.

"It's him," Cantore said. "Ninety percent certain."

"Who?"

"Dan Payne behind the wheel of that pickup truck. I sent those pictures to a guy who worked with him a few years back. Ninety percent certain. That's not absolute. But it's pretty good."

"I don't know," I said.

"And that truck is registered to a nonexistent address in Bay City, his old stomping grounds. It gets better. Reginald Reilly's got a bit of a record. It goes back almost 20 years."

"For what?"

"Here's the scary part. Pandering and contributing to the delinquency of a minor."

"He's a pimp?"

"Was. This was almost 20 years ago. He served two years. Then about four years back he was arrested for residential burglary. Guess who the arresting officer was?"

"You're kidding?"

"No. Our very own Dan Payne. And here's the funny thing, Reilly walked on the charge. That might lead you to believe that Payne cooked his testimony and now Reilly's repaying the favor."

"By lending him his truck."

"And who knows what else."

"So now what?"

"I'm still searching. I think I've got a line on a credit card for Reilly. That might give us something. We get enough, we'll take it to Detective Mulvey and talk him into doing his job."

"Did my ex-wife ever call?"

"Oh, yeah, tough lady. I answered a few of her questions and then asked some of my own. Funny thing, she didn't know a thing about her own hubby. So the conversation didn't last long."

When I got back to the classroom, Hotel Steve

was sound asleep. He looked right at home. He'd gotten his nickname by falling asleep in hotel lines.

The teacher was talking about uniforms. Should we be forced to wear them?

"Just be clean," a driver near the front said. "Take a shower now and then."

"We are like children without fathers," the guy next to me said.

"The customer wants something that looks familiar," the teacher said. "And if we don't clean up our act, the city might decide to put in a uniform code."

"For what?" a guy in front shouted. "To help the police capture the cabdriver?"

The class went on and on. Everybody agreed that the police picked on cabdrivers. Not a single driver admitted that he'd ever broken a traffic law.

"Don't deny. Don't argue," the teacher said. "Say 'I'm sorry. I didn't realize I did that.' Being tough with a cop does not enhance your manhood."

A few more drivers put their heads down on the table.

"The best way to avoid being robbed is to keep a clean cab," the teacher said. "If someone's looking to pull a robbery and sees your cab is super clean, he'll assume you just started and you won't have any money yet. He'll go find another cab to rob."

"You're giving a bunch of morons way too much credit," I said.

The teacher gave me a hard look but the guy next to me said, "Right you are, brother." He stuck out his fist and we bumped. "Right you are."

Nobody with any sense robbed cabs. There just

wasn't enough money in it for the risks involved. As far as I could tell, hardly anyone robbed cabs anymore. Back when Polack Lenny had been murdered, five or six drivers had been killed in robberies almost every year. I'd been against installing the bulletproof shields. But, I had to admit, they'd cut down on the slaughter.

"I had a very strange passenger," a small, soft-spoken guy said. "Can I tell you what happened."

"I'm almost afraid to ask," the teacher said.

The driver spoke for a good five minutes. I couldn't hear a word.

"Come on. Come on," the guy next to me said. "We're gonna be here 'til midnight."

The teacher pointed his finger at the soft-spoken driver. "That passenger owns the back seat of your cab from the time he gets in the back seat until the time he gets out. If he wants you to wait, you have to wait as long as he wants."

"Not in my cab," I said a bit too loudly.

"Mr. Miles all these rules apply to you as well."

When the class ended, I was the first one out the door.

FORTY-ONE

I'd just walked in the door at home when Cantore called. "Big news," he said. "I dug up a credit card for Reilly."

"Who?"

"Reginald Reilly. The guy that pickup truck is registered to. He only used it for gas at first. But boy was he in a hurry to get here. He gassed up in Kingman, Arizona about ten p.m. on the second and he was in Cuba, Missouri twenty hours later. That's 1450 miles. Add 300 miles, Kingman to L.A. That's almost 1800 miles."

"That's a lot of driving for one man," I said. "Maybe there was somebody with him."

"Sure. Like Dan Payne. You gotta add a couple of gas stops, too. So that truck was flying. But he didn't gas up in Illinois at all. The only reason we know he was here is that red light picture."

"Okay," I said. "I guess that photo was worth it."

"It's only 350 miles from Cuba to Chicago so he could have been here about three in the morning on the fourth."

"So that gives him a day to find Laura," I said. "But how does he do it?"

"You in the phone book?"

"I wanted Laura to be able to find me," I said.

"It could have happened that way. Or maybe Laura used your friend's phone to make a call or two. He might have followed you from Ace's."

"What does any of this prove? I can see you put some work in. But we already knew that truck was in Chicago. We knew it was from California. We still don't know if Payne was along for the ride."

"Hold on. It gets better," he said. "What time did you drop Laura off that night? One in the morning, right?"

"Something like that."

"Nine a.m. that pickup gases up in Iowa not quite 200 miles away."

"Okay. He's heading back west."

"Next stop Ogallala, Nebraska. He gassed up there at ten that night. Now his average speed's less than 50 miles an hour. Why?"

"Man's got to sleep sometime."

"Or maybe he doesn't want the police looking too closely at that truck."

I had a sudden image of Laura tied up in the back waiting for a chance to start kicking the walls.

"Next stop Greenville, Wyoming. It's a nothing town out in the middle of nowhere about 100 miles off the interstate."

"So why the stop?"

"Well, funny thing, there's a big wilderness camp in town."

"That's it!" I said, and I could feel a week's worth of tension slipping away. He wanted to re-program Laura, just like Wesley had suggested.

"Only problem is, the school looks totally straight. They don't take runaways or do drug treatment. Nothing like that. And they never heard of Laura."

"Yeah, but if they do that kind of stuff, why would they admit it?"

"Let me ask you this, if Laura did rip somebody off, you really think they're gonna punish her by sending her to camp?"

"Why else would they stop there?"

"I don't know," he said. "But I've checked the school out pretty thoroughly and it comes up clean. It's basically a rich kid's school. But that doesn't mean we shouldn't look a little closer. He stopped for some reason, stayed at the Stagecoach motel one night and then it was back to the interstate. But he was still taking his time. He gassed up in Evanston, Wyoming and then in Cedar City, Utah, which is south of Salt Lake. Then he stops in another motel in

Pearblossom, California. Funny thing, it's only 50-60 miles from home. If Dan Payne's behind the wheel, why would he stop when he was that close to home?"

"He finally ran out of steam," I suggested.

"Hell, if he needed a nap, he's got a camper back of that truck. And anyway, next night he's back to the same motel. So pretty long nap."

"So what's it mean?" I asked.

"I don't know," he said. "But you ever get to California, you can take a run out and see what you find. In the meantime, I'm putting together a file to take to Mulvey. I checked. He's working tonight. And that's it. There's not much more I can do from this end. We should settle up."

FORTY-TWO

Mike Cantore was once again hidden behind his desk lamp. "I can recommend a guy in L.A. I've used him before. But first take this to Mulvey."

"This" was a file folder containing all the information Cantore had been able to dig up on Dan Payne and Reginald Reilly. It included the credit card log, red-light photographs, driver's license photos, a photograph from Payne's days as a California cop, a newspaper story about Payne's resignation from the Bay City Police Department, and Reginald Reilly's rap sheet.

I took my time looking through it, comparing the police department photograph with the red light photos. It was impossible to say yes or no. The baseball cap didn't help matters.

The red light photographs showed the car before

it crossed into the intersection with the light already red, then moments later in the middle of the intersection. Only the first photo showed the driver. He was hunched over the steering wheel, his hands at the ten and two position, looking straight ahead. He didn't appear to notice the traffic signal at all.

Straight ahead was where you should look while driving, of course, with an occasional look in the rear view mirror and a glance from side to side now and then, especially when approaching an intersection. But this driver appeared locked in on something ahead of him. Maybe he was just tired. I'd been there myself plenty of times, just following the car in front, tired or lost in thought. It usually meant it was time to go home. But maybe he was so intent because his step-daughter was in that car up ahead.

"I don't understand why you can't come with me," I said.

"Cops don't like private eyes. It's really that simple."

"Yeah, but at least they'll listen to what you have to say. I'm just another mope to them."

"Yeah. But they're not really sure. You walk in with all this information, they know you got it somewhere but they don't know where. Which means you might be connected but they don't know how. They have to be nice, just in case. I'm with you, they know where the information came from. They know you're not connected."

"Why do I have to be connected in the first place," I said. "Shouldn't they be doing their job?"

"Eddie, you want to live in a dream world, go

ahead. Look, there's plenty of crime. Nobody's gonna go looking for more. Nobody. Mulvey's a good copper. They both are. If your friend had been shot or beaten, they'd be working the case. If someone had seen Laura being dragged away, kicking and screaming, they'd be on it. Believe me.

"I'm sure Payne grabbed her or had Reilly do it. It's really the only explanation. We don't know why he grabbed her. We don't know what he did with her. But, yeah, I'm convinced. But these guys need evidence or at least a reason to go looking for some."

"Maybe he really did drop her at one of those wilderness camps," I said. This was my one sliver of hope.

Cantore stuck his head out from behind the lamp. "You know what I'd do? If the cops won't help, I'd take a little road trip before all the tracks blow away. I'd stop in all those gas stations and motels and show that picture around. I'd go to Wyoming and check out that school. And I'd go to Pearblossom, too. And I'd ask around about wilderness camps. Who knows?"

"If they'd just tell me she was there. That'd be . . ." Just the thought almost brought me to tears.

"That'd be great, Eddie," he said. "That'd be great."

"Yeah."

"But one of the dangers of following someone's tracks, you might come face to face with him."

"That'd be okay with me," I said. "That'd be just fine."

"As long as you're prepared," he said. "You got a gun by any chance?"

I shook my head.

"Something to think about."

"They make me nervous," I said, and pulled out $1,700 and laid it on the desk top.

Cantore counted it, dropped it in a desk drawer, then stood up and came around the desk. "Let me know how it turns out," he said and opened the door. "And remember, I don't charge for advice, so don't be afraid to call."

We shook hands and said goodbye, then I walked down Harlem Avenue to Belmont and got on an eastbound bus. Several miles later it rumbled through the heart of Avondale. This is the neighborhood where I'd spent almost my entire married life. We'd lived a few blocks north of Belmont, first in an apartment, then in a small frame house.

Laura and I had driven by twice on our long tour. The second time we'd gotten out and walked down the narrow gangway. We'd stopped at the closed gate and looked into our old back yard.

"You promised me a dog," Laura had said. "Remember?"

"Yeah." We'd promised her a dog when we had a house and a yard of our own. And then we'd reneged.

FORTY-THREE

Detective Mulvey's eyes were as dead as the first time I'd seen them. He held up a single sheet of paper. "The autopsy report says heart attack. So there's really nothing to investigate."

"My daughter," I said.

150

"It's a mystery. I'll grant you that. But, you know, kids are funny. My guess, she found your friend dead and she didn't know what to do. So she panicked and took off."

"She panicked but she managed to take all her stuff?"

Mulvey shrugged.

"And isn't it a little strange that a guy her stepfather arrested ends up right behind us right before she disappears and leaves town right after?" I tried to catch his eyes, to let him know I knew he was full of shit, that he was just too lazy to do his job. But I couldn't find anything but a dull blackness.

"I wish I could help you, Mr. Miles. I really do."

"And all this." I gestured towards the file folder which contained all of Mike Cantore's information, information Mulvey had barely glanced at.

"You find me a crime that would be very interesting reading," he said. "Without one, it's just a lot of paper."

I picked up the folder and went out of the room and down the stairs.

"Eddie."

I turned and there was the sergeant with a group of cops around the front desk. He held up a single finger, said goodbye to the other cops, then came my way. "I'll walk out with you," he said. "What'd Mulvey say?"

"Ace died of a heart attack. There's nothing he can do."

"You ever call Cantore?"

I opened my file folder and pulled out the red-light photos. "That's either Laura's stepfather or some guy he once arrested running the light behind us at Peterson and Western the night she disappeared."

"That's dynamite. You sure?"

I started to tell him more. He stopped me and led me out to his car.

It was one of those short Cadillacs. I had to wait while he cleared off the passenger seat which was piled high with newspapers, magazines, and CDs. He transferred them to the back seat, where more of the same waited.

"Well, part of the mystery's solved," he said after I finished my story. "It's the evil step-father. So what now?"

"I'm thinking of driving out there," I said. "You know, retrace his steps. Show that picture around. Go to that wilderness camp. See if there's one in Pearblossom. Maybe talk to the police out there or another private detective. Cantore's got a guy he uses. I'm not sure yet."

"Pearblossom," he said. "That's my bet."

"You know it?"

"There's nothing to know. It's the middle of nowhere. One of my ex's was a Santa Barbara girl. That's the shortcut to Vegas. Pearblossom Highway. You've got your work cut out for you, Eddie. It's nothing but desert and mountains and a million hiding places. Hold on a sec."

He got out and opened the trunk and came back with a road atlas. He turned the light on then opened the atlas to the Southern California page. "Right there," he said. He pointed to a tiny dot above the name Pearblossom.

Pearblossom Highway was an east-west road, a narrow line through a large, blank space. Edwards Air Force base was a few inches north, metropolitan Los Angeles was about the same distance south, on the other side of the San Gabriel Mountains. There were several lakes north of Pearblossom. According to the map all of them were dry.

"So yeah, retrace his steps," the sergeant said. "Maybe that'll give you a feel for him. But if he's holding her against her will, odds are it's somewhere around Pearblossom. If he killed her, and you've got to consider that possibility, she might be buried out that way.

"If she's in one of those wilderness camps she's gonna turn up sooner or later. I wouldn't waste much time with that. You any good at disguises?"

"I always just bought a mask on Halloween."

"You're gonna need more than that. Think you can look like a cowboy?"

"I can try."

"You gotta figure he's dangerous and he might be waiting for you. You're gonna be on his territory. So you gotta at least try to blend in."

"Blue jeans and cowboy boots."

"Something like that," he said. "You get out there, check the local look. But Payne's gonna be tough no matter what you're wearing. You got a gun, Eddie?"

I shook my head. "Cantore just asked me the same question."

"This might be the time to pick one up," he said. "Something serious. You know damn well Payne's armed."

"Maybe," I said.

"Start with this Reilly guy. That's what I'd do. He's a pimp and a burglar. Those are both cowardly professions. He probably won't give you too much trouble. Yeah, he might be your way in. Use him to figure out how to get to Payne."

"I don't know," I said.

"I'm not too worried about you, Eddie. You did it once. Remember that. William Calloway killed what, seven cabbies? But he couldn't kill you."

"He came close."

"Don't mean a thing," he said. "You know that first day at your friend's house, some reason you really got to me. You were like a bull all ready to charge but you didn't have the first idea which way to go. I said to myself, here's a man who loves his little girl."

"You're the only one who gave a shit."

He shrugged. "I had a daughter," he said. "Emily. She hated me for some reason. Never did understand it. Typical cop's kid. She broke every law she could think of, took every drug she could find. Well, you know how that ended."

"Sorry."

He turned his head and gave me a long look. "I buried him." I didn't ask but he answered just the same. "The guy she was with that night. It probably wasn't even his fault but I had to do something." He held my eyes. "I probably shouldn't be telling you this."

I shrugged. "Why not?"

"You don't get your little girl back," he said in a whisper, "you bury this Payne cocksucker." He held

154

my eyes for a long moment. "It won't bring her back but it'll sure do wonders for your heartache."

FORTY-FOUR

It rained all the next day. I couldn't get myself out of the house.

Who was I kidding, anyway? I wasn't a detective. I wasn't a tough guy. I wasn't going to bury Dan Payne. So now I was going to drive across the country and do what? Probably nothing much. But even that was better than doing nothing at all.

I called around looking for a rental car. It was hold music and confusion. How long would I want the car? Would I be returning it to the same location? Did I want a green car? "I don't care what color it is," I said the first time I answered the question.

Eventually, I found an umbrella and walked the two miles down to the roundtable.

There wasn't a single cab parked out front. I sat down by myself and ordered a complete dinner; meatloaf, green beans, mashed potatoes and gravy, a salad, rice pudding and coffee. And I finished it all and asked for a refill on the coffee.

I missed Claire, who had been the overnight waitress here for years. We'd talked about anything and everything. She was one of the few people I could be completely honest with. If it was the old days, she'd be sitting across from me, and I wouldn't have to pretend to be brave, like I did for the sergeant.

I missed Ace, too. He could always read my moods. He knew when I was down and he always

155

helped me talk it out.

Not-So-Fat Wally came in after a while. He went back out for his computer, and then started looking for rent-a-car deals.

Wally found me a car, unlimited miles, $155 a week.

"I've got no idea how long it's gonna take," I said. "But it's probably going to be longer than a week."

Ken Willis and Paki Bob showed up next. "Why don't you see if you can borrow Ace's car?" Willis suggested.

"That's not a bad idea," I said, and I pulled out my phone.

"Eddie!" Kenny stopped me before I got far. "You can't call Ace's daughter at one in the morning."

The conversation shifted to medallion prices. They'd been going up about a thousand dollars a day. Paki Bob was already regretting selling too soon.

"I should have waited," he said.

"You want all the money in the world?" Wally asked.

"Isn't that the idea?" Paki said.

"I don't get it," Wally said. "Why do they keep going up?"

"Supply and demand," Willis said. "For some crazy reason people want to drive cabs."

"Hell, you don't need a medallion for that," Wally said.

"The real estate market is in the toilet," Paki said. "The banks aren't paying any interest. If you've got cash, it's one of the few places you might actually make something with your money."

"Remember what happened after 9/11." Willis said. Medallion prices had fallen that day, and it had taken years for them to recover.

"That's not going to happen again," Paki said.

"Maybe you should call Homeland Security, let 'em know."

It was just like the old days sitting around the roundtable. Everybody with an opinion. Everybody with something to say. It was as if nothing had happened. As if everything was still the same.

Nobody spoke Laura's name until Wesley came in. "Any luck?" he asked.

I shook my head, and a few minutes later said goodbye.

Ken Willis gave me a ride home.

"Kenny, I don't know anything except that the stepfather grabbed her."

"What are you planning to do out there?

"Whatever it takes," I said.

"You want to borrow my .38?"

"I thought you got rid of that thing."

"Never. I stopped carrying it in the cab. But I'm just like Ace. It's right there in the nightstand."

"Fat lot of good it did him."

FORTY-FIVE

In the morning, I called Ace's daughter Marilyn.

"I was wondering if I could borrow your father's car for a while," I said.

"Hmmm," she murmured. "Let me call Irene and I'll call you right back."

I disconnected the call. Well, that's that, I thought.

But a few minutes later she actually did call back. "You can pick it up this morning," she said. "Irene's at the house now. We were planning to give it to charity. But if you can use it, we'd just as soon give it to you."

"Really? That'd be great."

"Dad talked about you often," she said. "Has there been any news from Laura?"

"Nothing."

"I'm sorry to hear that. Well, good luck, Eddie. If there's anything else we can do, please let us know."

There's never a cab around when you want one. I walked up Lincoln to the el station and took the Western Avenue bus to Ace's.

"The place is in turmoil," Irene said when she opened the door. "Would you like a cup of tea?"

"Oh, sure," I said, and she led me into the kitchen.

There were packing boxes everywhere, opened and closed. But there were still two spaces at the big kitchen table.

"Most of it's going to charity," Irene said. "So if you see anything you'd like let me know."

"Are you really giving me the car?" I hadn't owned a car since my days as a pizza delivery man.

"Certainly," she said. "Now, here are the keys and here's the title. The insurance card is in the glove compartment and it's paid up until the end of June, so you don't have to worry about insurance until then."

"I don't know how to thank you."

"The gas tank is almost full. The oil was changed just last month. There's a spare tire in the trunk, I think it needs a bit of air. And there's a flashlight and some tools and maps in the glove compartment."

"You remind me of your father," I said.

"Thank you. People have always said we were the most alike." She stood up and picked something off the top of a carton. "I believe this was Laura's," she said, and she laid a pink book on the table between us. "We found it under the sofa in the den."

"It sure looks like hers," I said. I picked it up, unzipped it, and flipped through the pages without really looking at the words. "It's hers all right."

"I found it the other day," she said. "I didn't know what it was so I had to look inside, of course. I considered not giving it to you. But I talked it over with Marilyn and we decided we should give it to you. But I must warn you, it's rather racy."

"Racy?" I said.

"Maybe I should say explicit."

"Oh." I understood that.

"So if you decide to read it, try to remember that we were all young once. And we all experimented with this and that. And we've all done things we've come to regret."

"You're scaring me to death here," I said.

"I just want you to be prepared."

"Well, thanks," I said. "You know your father said something the night Laura came. He said we were idiots at that age. Look at the world today. They're gonna be even bigger idiots."

"I think that sums it up nicely," she said.

FORTY-SIX

I stopped at home for my suitcase then at the bank for a pile of cash. Before long, I was on the East-West Tollway in the heart of the Western suburbs following the signs for Interstate 88.

Traffic thinned out beyond Aurora and the road narrowed. Soon it was farm country and the speed limit jumped to 65, ten miles over the Chicago limit. It was a sunny winter day. Patches of snow were scattered over brown fields. Spring was just days away.

I pulled into a service area outside of DeKalb. My trip odometer said I'd gone 67 miles. I kicked the tires and checked the oil. The spare tire was low, just as Irene had said. I topped it off, got coffee and cookies at the McDonald's and carried them back to the car. It felt good to be actually going somewhere.

I opened my road atlas, a gift from the sergeant. I-88 only went as far as the Quad Cities. This is where I would pick up Interstate 80 and cross the Mississippi into Iowa.

I closed the atlas and picked up Laura's pink book and started paging through it. I hadn't gone far when I remembered Irene's warning.

Can you have an orgy with just one other person? Sure can! OMG! Scott is better than Ken, Larry and Mike combined. OMG!

I closed the book--zipped it shut and stashed it in the glove box--then got back on the highway. I pulled up to yet another tollbooth and held two dollars out the window.

"It's $3.60," the woman in the cage said.

"It was only a buck and a half last time."

"Sir, I don't set the price."

A few miles later I glanced at the speedometer. I was doing an even 90, twenty-five over the limit. I took my foot off the gas and drifted into the right lane.

The sun was winter bright and before long I was driving straight into it. I lowered the sun visor but the road was shimmering from edge to edge. My sunglasses were home in my cab-driving bag. I reached over and opened the glove compartment and felt around. No sunglasses. I pulled out Laura's book and sat it on the seat beside me.

"It's okay, Laura," I said. "It's okay."

FORTY-SEVEN

By the time I crossed the Mississippi the sun was almost gone. Iowa looked like Illinois with more hills and trucks. The speed limit jumped to 70.

Interstate 80 was the cross-country route between New York City and San Francisco. I slipped in behind an Allied Van Lines rig--the rear of the trailer plastered with snow--and tried to enjoy riding along. For years, I'd had daydreams about getting out on the highway.

I'd even been tempted by truck driving school. "Learn to drive the big rigs!" the radio used to shout. One day while down in the dumps I'd actually called the 800 number. I didn't sign up but that didn't stop the dreaming.

The pickup truck's first gas stop had been at a

truck stop 180 miles west of Chicago. The billboard said, "World's Largest Truck Stop." It was a sprawling place and I knew, before I walked inside, that no one would remember Dan Payne or Reginald Reilly, whoever I was following. I talked to pump jockeys and waitresses, and nobody even thought the man in the photograph looked familiar.

"You the police?" the manager asked.

"Just a father."

I picked up a pocket-size notebook in the travel store and then showed the same picture to the cashier.

She barely looked. "You know how many people I see?"

"I was just asking about this one." I grabbed the notebook and my coffee to go, got back on the highway, and slipped into the rhythm of the road.

As it got later, most of the cars disappeared. Soon the highway was almost nothing but trucks. They flashed their headlights as passing trucks cleared, blinked their trailer lights as they pulled back into the stream.

I was cruising a bit over the speed limit. During the day, I'd been passing most of the trucks. Now most of them were passing me. They came by in flocks; six or ten at a time, out in the left lane, going faster and faster as the night went on, highballing along.

I looked over as a gleaming blue truck nosed past. Salinas, California, the sign on the passenger door said. I glanced up. A woman with long blond hair had a leg stretched out to the dashboard. She turned and caught me looking, flashed a smile and the peace sign, and was gone in a blast of noise, light, and glittering chrome.

I pulled in behind the last truck in the pack and found myself singing "I wish they all could be California girls." But then I caught myself. There was only one girl I cared about, and she'd always be a Chicago girl to me.

We went through Council Bluffs and Omaha. We were in Nebraska now and the speed limit jumped again, this time to 75.

This was the way to travel, I decided, as we cruised along. No starting and stopping. No red lights. No one in the back seat.

As it got later and later, the trucks began to spread out a bit. My coffee buzz began to wane. I turned the radio on for the first time and hit the scan button then stopped at a country voice.

Lights flashing, trucks passing
in that beautiful roar
the highway whispers
an old truck driving song

I listened for that highway whisper and when I found it, it almost lulled me to sleep. Somewhere past Lincoln I saw a sign for a Super 8 Motel and pulled off. I'd driven 600 miles. That was enough for the first day.

I carried my bag into the room then walked across to the adjacent restaurant. After a bowl of soup and a sandwich, I stopped at the car and picked up the road atlas and Laura's book.

I took a shower, flipped through the channels on

163

the television, then decided to take another peek. I started at the beginning.

> *Another try at a diary. Maybe if I tell the Truth it will be easier. Here's my belated resolutions!! No more sympathy xx's. I always feel so bad afterwards and they always want more. Always! Always! Always! Am I so good or just too easy?*

> *No more MAS except on weekends! Must do all homework--even for Mr. Creepy Pants.*
> *Lose 2 pounds. Hot! Hot! Hot!*
> *Hook up with Scott #1 or Mick #2! Don't forget to talk to Ellen. But what if she says no?*

I decided not to turn the page. I already knew how this particular chapter turned out.

I remembered Ace dictating to Laura and flipped ahead until I found it.

> *NEVER MESS WITH ANOTHER MAN'S MONEY!*
> *Ace says this is one of life's most important rules. Too late for me!!! Too bad.*

Well at least there was no sex, I decided, as I skimmed through pages where Laura listed all our purchases. She spent almost an entire page describing the leather jacket. And then there I was:

> *Real dad is so N-O-R-M-A-L! Can't believe Mighty Mom ever hooked up with him.*

Mighty Mom, that brought my first laugh in days. I turned a few more pages and there I was again:

Feel more like MM's blood for sure.
RD is not the Super Dad I was hoping for.
He won't even look me in the eyes.
If I told him the truth, he'd probably puke.
He won't pick anybody up unless they look like a
banker or a lawyer. And I thought he was going to
save me!

That was enough for the night, I decided. I dropped the book to the bottom of my suitcase.

Save you from what? Why didn't you ever tell me?

FORTY-EIGHT

I spent the next day driving across Nebraska looking for people. Where was everyone? The fields were spotted with snow but no people. The only signs of life were on the highway where a steady stream of cars and trucks moved in both directions. Were the farmers sharpening their tools while their wives knitted?

I stopped at a rest area and the wind was so strong it was a battle making it from the car to the washroom. Had everyone blown away?

A snow plow sat on the shoulder, lights flashing. Farther along a sign warned, "I-80 CLOSED AHEAD WHEN FLASHING. PREPARE TO EXIT." There were railroad-style crossing gates on either side of the highway. But the lights were not flashing. The gates were up.

A pump jockey in Ogallala thought he might

have seen the pickup truck. It had gone straight from the gas pumps to the phone booth. The driver had then spent an hour or more either on the phone or pacing around the truck, opening and closing various doors. This odd behavior was probably the reason the kid remembered the truck. He thought there might have been someone sitting in the passenger seat. But he was pretty sure it was another guy. "I would have remembered a pretty girl," he said.

I followed the same path the pickup had taken. It wasn't a real phone booth, of course, just a three-sided shelter that would keep your torso out of the wind. If the wind happened to be blowing in the right direction.

The phone, walls, and counter were all covered with pen marks and knife engravings. Most of it was illegible or of the standard for-a-good-time variety. But someone had boxed out a small area in the center of the counter and two ten digit numbers were written in black ink. Nobody had yet scrawled anything on top.

I opened my notebook and copied the numbers to page one.

That night I stayed in Cheyenne, Wyoming. Just the name brought back memories of old Westerns. Wasn't there a big Army fort here in the cowboy-and-Indian days? Maybe it was a railroad town. I didn't get far enough from the motel to find out. It was just another town along the highway now.

In the morning, I picked up coffee and a roll in the motel lobby and was soon back on the road.

Now I was in the West and, if things went right, by the end of the day, I would be further west than I'd ever gotten.

"STRONG WINDS," a sign along the highway warned. "ADVISE NO LIGHT TRAILERS."

The last hundred miles to Greenville, Wyoming, was mountain two-lane. This was the west you dream about. The road curved around going up and down snow-covered mountains, then ran straight as could be through the valleys. Nobody passed in the valleys, of course. They waited for the mountains, then whizzed around me doing 80 while I gripped the steering wheel and tried not to look down.

5300, the population sign said. There was snow on the ground. The main street was clear but the side streets were snow packed.

The motel where Reginald Reilly had stayed was on the main drag. A bell rang when I opened the door. The desk clerk was an older woman, dressed in blue and yellow. She smiled and said hello then hesitated when I showed her the red light photograph. "Well, he was here all right," she said after a bit, "but I don't know if Mr. Parenti would approve of me talking to you."

"That's the boss?"

"Is he ever."

"Maybe I could talk to him," I said.

"He's about halfway to Laramie by now."

"Well, look, I'm pretty sure this guy kidnapped my daughter. I know he stopped here but that's really all I know. So anything you can tell me would help. Did he have a young girl with him? She's eighteen. Did you see her? You should be able to tell me that much."

"I knew you weren't the police," she said.

"No."

"He was a very nice fellow. But I guess that ain't true if he kidnapped your girl. But he was talkative. That's probably why I remember him. And of course we don't have that many guests this time of year."

"What did he talk about?"

"You know, I don't really remember."

"Did you see a young girl with him?"

"No. It was just him and his friend."

"There was another guy with him?"

"Oh, yes, definitely."

"What'd he look like, the other guy?"

"Well, to be honest, I couldn't tell you which one is in your picture. They looked a bit like brothers. I think I assumed they were."

"There's supposed to be a wilderness camp around here."

"That's what we're known for," she said, and she gave me directions to the school. It was five minutes away, clear on the other side of town.

"We don't give out information on our students," the woman behind the desk at the Leadership School said. She looked a bit like my favorite teacher, Mrs. Vallo from sixth grade. Maybe that's why I believed her every word. "Could I ask why you think she might be here?"

"Well, she was pretty much kidnapped by her stepfather. They stayed overnight at the Stagecoach Motel and asked about schools or camps. And you're the biggest one in the area."

"We are certainly that," she said. "And we've been

here for more than forty years. But we're not a therapeutic camp. We don't take kidnapped children. We don't do drug treatment or anything of that nature. We don't have psychiatrists on staff. We're a wilderness camp. But we don't do wilderness therapy. Do you know if they stopped in Utah, by any chance?"

"That's where he went after here."

"Then that's probably where you'll find your daughter."

"Only problem is, they stopped here. Not there."

"Well, I can tell you this, Mr. Miles. Our last class started three weeks ago. But I'm certain there is no one named Payne or Miles enrolled."

She walked to a file cabinet, opened the top drawer, and pulled out a stack of thin folders, maybe twenty in all, and returned to the front counter and started shuffling through them.

"Let's see. No. No Payne or Miles. Only three girls and I can assure you that none of them sounds anything like your daughter." She pulled out three files, one at a time, laid them on the counter and then opened them so I could easily see the photographs clipped to the inside cover. None of them were of Laura. "I'm sorry," she said. "That's really more information than I'm allowed to give out."

I pushed the red light photograph across the counter. "Does he look familiar?"

"No. I don't believe so." She picked up the photograph and took a closer look. "You know, I think he might have come in one day." She gestured towards the stack of brochures down the counter.

"I'm almost certain. I was on the phone. He just picked up a brochure and waved goodbye."

"Thank you so much," I said. Maybe Dan Payne had realized this wasn't the place for his kidnapped daughter, and continued west.

"Good luck," the woman said.

On the way out the door, I grabbed a copy of the same brochure then sat behind the wheel paging through it.

It looked nothing like any school I'd ever attended. The students were on skis and on horseback, climbing mountains and paddling canoes, without a city or a highway anywhere in sight. In one photograph desert flowers bloomed, another showed a mountain stream cutting through pure white snow.

All the students looked happy and well adjusted. None looked like they'd been kidnapped or forced to attend.

I turned a page and then stopped. It wasn't Laura but it was close enough that I heard myself say hello. The girl was in climbing gear, halfway up a golden-brown mountain. She'd stopped to give the photographer a goofy grin. She didn't look tired. She looked strong and determined. I had no doubt that she'd get to the top.

It would be just one adventure in a long, eventful life, I thought, and closed my eyes and tried to imagine Laura in a similar pose. But I couldn't do it. I couldn't see her anywhere near this school. "Lucky rich kids," I said, and closed the book.

When I opened my eyes, I found myself looking at a familiar phone number on the brochure's back cover. I pulled out my notebook and found the same number there. It was one of two numbers I'd copied from that gas station phone booth in Ogallala.

I tossed the brochure on the back seat and before long I was back on Interstate 80. But now I knew for certain that I was following two men. One of them had to be Dan Payne.

"ROAD CLOSED WHEN FLASHING," a sign warned. But, once again, the lights were off and the gates were standing open.

FORTY-NINE

I continued on trying to remember my own wild and crazy youth.

The kinkiest moment I could come up with was standing with my on-again/off-again girlfriend Karen, watching my best friend Matt and his girl Ellie having a ball.

We'd been down the hall in the other bedroom when Karen and I decided we wanted to swap partners. This is something we did regularly for a year or so.

Karen and I had a good time watching, and playing around while waiting for them to finish. For years, I'd fantasized that we'd all gotten together that day but we never had.

We shared one-bed motel rooms a few times. But one couple always slept on the floor. One morning I woke to find myself on the floor alone. Both girls were in bed with Matt, one in each arm. They were all asleep and Matt had a very contented look on his face but I never did find out if I'd missed anything.

Matt joined the Army not long afterwards, and

the girls drifted away. And that was as close as I ever got to an orgy except in my imagination.

So I guess that made me N-O-R-M-A-L. But isn't that what parents are supposed to be? Mine certainly were.

Matt and I had once started for California on the old Route 66. We spent a very long weekend in Amarillo, Texas, and then had gone on to New Mexico nursing hangovers. When we counted our money in Santa Rosa, we realized we barely had enough to get back home. We'd turned around and that was as far west as I'd ever gotten.

Maybe that was my life. Was I destined to never finish anything? I hadn't finished college, my marriage, my career as a project manager or raising my daughter.

But I was going to finish this time. I would either find Laura or I would find out what happened to her. And I remembered the sergeant's not-so-subtle advice. I still couldn't see myself burying anyone. I'd give it a try if I ever got the chance. But first I had to get the diary out of my mind. Pretend Laura was my son. Would I care as much if he'd mentioned something vague about an orgy? And who knew what Laura meant by that word? When I was a kid I thought a French kiss was some kind of oral sex. And the closest I'd ever come to an orgy was fantasy. Maybe it was the same for Laura.

I couldn't quite talk myself into that, any more than I could talk myself into believing that all kids thought their parents were boring cowards. But I kept remembering Ace's words: We were idiots. They'd be even bigger ones.

FIFTY

A pump jockey in Evanston, Wyoming, remembered the pickup truck. But when I asked a few questions, it turned out that it looked exactly like a friend's truck, and that was about all he remembered. If there were wilderness camps in the area, no one at the gas station was talking.

The long descent into Salt Lake City made me realize how lucky I was that the weather was agreeable.

Most of the trucks crept along with their flashers going. I could almost feel the tension as I passed. It felt like we were driving down from the top of the Sears Tower. There was a runaway truck ramp off to the left. I wondered how often that got used.

I stopped for the night in Cedar City, a bit shy of the Arizona line. This was another of the pickup truck's gas stops.

"He was in that movie, right?" the desk clerk at the motel said when I showed her the red light photograph.

I found an old Western on TV but fell asleep before too long. I woke with an announcer shouting that operators were standing by. I reached out, pushed the power button and was soon dreaming.

The woman from the Leadership School was behind a desk. No. It wasn't her. It was my old sixth grade teacher, Mrs. Vallo. I was passing hand-drawn cartoons back and forth with my friend Bob. We did this all day long and Mrs. Vallo usually pretended not to see.

Laura was sitting across the aisle. We were in

173

sixth grade together. She leaned close. "Dad, you don't have to worry about me," she whispered.

"Laura, would you like to share that with the class?" Mrs. Vallo said. She had eyes in the back of her head and was always tougher on the girls.

"I'm sorry, Mrs. Vallo," Laura said. "I was just telling Eddie his shoelace was undone."

"Edwin, would you please tie your shoe so Laura can sit still." Mrs. Vallo said. "Now where was I?"

I bent down to tie my laces but I wasn't wearing shoes. I had the feet of a grown man.

I turned the lights on and picked up Laura's book. I started at the beginning. I would read it as if Laura was my son, and I would try not to look down on his good time.

I read on and on, wincing now and then at a young girl's adventure with romance, friends, schools and drugs. MAS, I discovered, was an abbreviation for "mind altering substances." ESD stood for "evil step dad." MM was "Mighty Mom." I was RD, short for "real dad."

I came to the part just before her arrival in Chicago.

> Rents are taking a second honeymoon in
> Rio w/o me. Not fair. Instead I get to stay in
> the big new house all by myself. Big deal.
> I probably won't even like it. ESD says I should
> be thankful no babysitter. Very funny. No more
> than one guest at a time. No sleepovers.
> No boys in bedroom! Even funnier!!!

174

Two pages later:

Stupidest house ever. Not even a chair
downstairs.
No time to write--too busy pretend
Honeymoon with Scott. True honey. He
likes everything. Me too! Forever!!!

There was a long series of hearts. But then the fun and games stopped. The next four pages were filled top to bottom with OMG! OMG! It went on and on. *Oh my god!*

ESD is pure devil---worse than devil. OMG!
That's why there's no furniture.
Scott says if this gets out we can forget about
college or anything. I'm having a breakdown!!
Did MM know?? No. I'll never believe it!!
She wouldn't would she? Devil! Devil! Devil!
Even worse than I thought.

I read it over and over but I couldn't make sense of it. What the hell had happened? What had Payne done? And what had happened to the furniture? I turned the page.

Scott made copies of everything. Then we
wrecked the devil's domain. Scott tore
all the computers apart, took out the
hard drives--then smashed them good.

*Found $48,000 inside one computer. Scott
says this proves the existence of God. I say
it proves ESD is the devil for sure.
We're taking it where he'll never find us.
Scott went home to pack.*

*Everything went wrong! Scott dropped me at
Safeway and went to get gas. When I came out with
the groceries the police had him pulled over.
He never once looked my way. They put him in the
back of the cop car and drove away.
A tow truck took my car.*

*On a bus to Chicago. Only thing I could think of.
Try to find real dad. Maybe he'll help---if I
can even tell him!!!!*

*Chicago is such an old city! I hardly remember.
Waiting for real dad to show up. With his
friend Ace. He's older than dirt but pretty
cool. Can't wait to meet RD--sounds like
just the man I need!!!!*

*NEVER MESS WITH ANOTHER MAN'S
MONEY.*

"Just the man I need," I said, and I remembered
Ace saying how he and Ken Willis had built me up
as a hero.

I turned the TV on, anything but being alone with
my thoughts. The room was much too small. I got
dressed, grabbed my jacket, and started walking.

Before long, the houses stopped, the street ended.
A well-traveled path continued on into the darkness

of the woods. But I could see light on the other side. I stumbled along and came into a small clearing, a meadow. The light was the moon shining down from a star-filled sky.

I didn't know what Payne had done but whatever it was, it was enough to let a couple of kids easily justify stealing $48,000. How would Payne respond to that? He couldn't call the police. Not if it was drug money. Had he murdered Scott? Would he do the same to a girl he'd helped raise?

Payne wasn't her real father, of course. She wasn't his blood. She was mine. But I'd deserted her years ago, and then when she'd come looking for help, I'd treated her like a tourist out to see the big town.

I lay on my back in that cold, damp meadow, and watched the sky. I hadn't seen stars like this in years. There must be a god and heaven up there behind all that drifting stardust. Hell was right here.

FIFTY-ONE

There was a backup leading to the inspection station at the California state line. No. I did not have any fruits or vegetables, I said, and they waved me though. The speed limit dropped to 70.

Two hours later, I followed a sign which said "Victorville," and headed west towards Pearblossom. At first, the highway was divided with two lanes in each direction. It wasn't nearly as remote as the sergeant had led me to believe.

Before long it was full night and two lanes merged into one. With the exception of a few scattered lights and the occasional car, there was nothing but darkness here. This wasn't the end of the world but it might as well have been. Los Angeles was just over the mountains on my left, 25 or 30 miles due south if you happened to be a bird. Driving, it was a much longer trip. Was Pearblossom Highway some familiar short cut for Payne? I wondered. A way to avoid the traffic of Los Angeles.

"Speed Zone Ahead," a sign warned. The next one said: "Pearblossom."

The Starlight Motel sign needed more than a few replacement bulbs. But the VACANCY sign was burning bright. There were two gas stations, a restaurant and that was it. The town was gone. I made a U-turn. A couple of pick up trucks were parked in front of the restaurant but neither matched the truck from the red light photograph.

The motel was tiny, maybe a dozen rooms. I rang the bell. A sign said, "If no answer, try the cafe." An arrow pointed towards the restaurant.

Curtains at the back of the office parted and a guy in jeans, T-shirt, and a leather vest, stepped through. He unlocked the door. "Howdy," he said. "You looking for a room?"

"Yep," I said.

"Forty-five for one bed. Fifty-five for two."

"Just one," I said. I filled in the card and counted out $45.

I laid the red light photograph on the counter between us. "You ever seen this guy?" I asked.

He didn't even glance at the photograph. "I couldn't say."

"Look, he kidnapped my daughter," I said, and I pulled out a twenty and folded it a few times until it fit snugly in the palm of my hand. "I know he stayed here. Here." I reached out.

"No. It's okay," he said. "Yeah, he was here the other week alright. He's stayed other times too. He's a mountain climber or a desert rat. Maybe both. I'm not sure."

"Where is the desert, anyway?"

"That's the Mojave Desert right out the door," he said. "They call this the Antelope Valley. But as far as I'm concerned it's desert. High desert."

"So what does a desert rat do?"

"Oh, they go racing around in their trucks and ATVs, hunting for kangaroo rats or prospecting for gold. They drive like idiots and go off the trails and they make new trails and then the water follows along and that destroys whatever vegetation there is. If they keep it up there won't be any animals left to chase. Most of 'em are just crazy fools, you ask me."

"There's gold out here?"

"Now if I thought that, you think I'd be in here?"

I held up the photograph. "You remember anything special about him?"

"Not really. I checked him in--for one night--and then I'm pretty sure he was back the next night, too."

"You see a teenage girl with him?"

He shook his head. "Sorry."

"Did you talk to him?"

"Well, sure. But just howdy-do. Nothing beyond that."

"Are there any wilderness schools in town?"

"Mister, we don't even have a high school."

I said thanks, got back in the car and drove down to the room. It wasn't a Super 8 but it wasn't a dump either.

I took a cool shower then tried to watch TV. That lasted about five minutes and then I was in my jacket and out the door.

The sign had gone out in the restaurant. Lights were still burning inside. I followed a sidewalk until that crumbled away to nothing, and then continued along on a foot path along the edge of the road. This was the middle of nowhere that the sergeant had talked about. A few lights shone here and there in the distance but only a few. Every so often a car raced past, kicking up dust. One driver tapped the horn.

I came to three crosses. Burnt-out candles and empty beer cans were scattered on the ground beneath them, along with what looked like a tiny dashboard statue. The crosses were pushed back on an angle as if they'd been sideswiped. Wind-blown garbage had joined the mementoes.

What was I doing out here? What would I see with no light?

I turned around, but instead of going back to my room, I got in the car and headed west.

FIFTY-TWO

Before too long the speed limit and the traffic increased, the highway added a lane, and Palmdale came into view. It wasn't much. But there were street lights and flashing signs, fast food joints and other assorted signs of life. It was the heart of the Loop compared to Pearblossom.

I switched over to Route 14 and for the first time in 2000 miles I was in real traffic. You could almost smell Los Angeles from here. We were cutting through mountains but everybody was driving as if we were on the salt flats. Reflectors were imbedded between the lanes. They gave the highway a hallucinatory feel. I tried to stay over to the right and out of everyone's way but it was impossible not to speed. It was impossible not to drift on to the reflectors which doubled as rumble strips.

This is where Laura had learned to drive, I realized. She must have seen Chicago traffic as a picnic.

Chatsworth could have been any of the post-war Chicago suburbs. There was too much traffic, wide streets with shopping and more shopping and enough parking spaces for every car in America. Only the outcasts walked. But even they knew where they were going.

After several minutes of wandering around lost, I got into the rhythm of the place. It didn't take me too long to find Revere Street or 421, the new house that Dan Payne had bought to lure Laura and Susan back to his side.

It was one of the larger houses on the block, two stories, white with blue trim. The only lights were above the front door and on either side of the attached three-car garage. It looked like a thousand other suburban homes.

I drove past and around the block looking for an alley but there wasn't one. Revere was entirely residential and there weren't any obvious hiding places. Only a few cars were parked at the curb.

There were several FOR SALE signs. The house at 460 looked to be vacant. The grass was overgrown. Advertising circulars were stuck on the front door. I backed into the driveway, killed my lights, and sat looking at the house down the block. Nothing was happening. It was nine o'clock on a suburban evening. From the lights flickering in various windows it looked like many of the neighbors were watching TV. But there were no flickers in the house I cared about, the house that Laura and Scott had run from.

I rolled the window down, stuck my arm out and felt a gentle breeze. It must have been sixty. This was the first time I'd noticed the weather in days.

I sat there for a while and then drifted into a comfortable sleep. When I woke it was almost two in the morning. The house down the block was still dark. So were most of its neighbors.

Had Dan Payne come or gone while I was dreaming?

FIFTY-THREE

It was still dark when I awoke in my Pearblossom motel room. *Could Laura have been in that house last night?* I hadn't even tried the door.

When I came out of the shower the sun was coming up. I dressed in jeans and a flannel shirt, then sat on the edge of the bed and dialed Susan's number. I left my message after the beep. "Hey, it's Eddie. I'm out here. Give me a call."

I put my bag in the trunk of the car then walked to the front office. The door was locked. A handwritten note said: "Back about noon. If you can't wait go to the cafe and ask them to call me." I dropped my key in a slot on the door, and then went to the cafe and ordered breakfast.

The place was made up to look authentically Western. But the last remodel had been long ago. The walls were hung with oversized photographs of famous actors--John Wayne, Robert Mitchum, James Arness--and novelty signs about miners and street girls. But everything was covered in a thin layer of dust. A new coat of paint wouldn't hurt. Something to hide the drabness, the years of grease. The floor needed a good wax job, the tabletops varnish. A few live-movie-star pictures might help, too.

A ten-stool counter was laid out with coffee cups, napkins and silverware. I joined a couple of guys who were head down over their coffees and turned my cup over.

The waitress came by with the coffee pot, smiled, filled my cup, then went down the counter and topped the other two. She put the coffee pot away then dropped a menu in front of me.

"So, hon, how you all?" She was a shapely brunette with a nice smile.

"Hungry," I said. I'd been eating nothing but garbage for days.

"Well, you've come to the right place," she said. "Special today is rattlesnake stew."

"I was thinking of breakfast. Over easy, bacon, toast."

She wrote that down. "I was just kidding about that stew," she said.

I swiveled around. There was an older couple at

one table. They looked as Midwestern as me. Three cowboys were sitting right under the James Arness photograph. I remembered the sergeant's advice to dress local. The cowboys were all young, all in jeans and cowboy boots. Two of them were wearing vests. I was trying to figure out if they were wearing snap button shirts when I felt their eyes on me.

I smiled and pointed at James Arness. "Gunsmoke," I said, and quickly swiveled back around.

Between the restaurant and the motel a sign pointed south: DEVIL'S PUNCHBOWL NATURAL AREA. The landscape was rugged but there were plenty of trees. Many of the scattered houses would have looked right at home in any upscale suburb.

I followed signs up the mountain and eventually pulled into a parking area and walked to a scenic lookout. The mountainside was strewn with huge boulders and massive rocks. It was the perfect place for an outlaw hideout in some old Western. The posse would never get their horses through the jumbled maze. Down the mountain the land flattened out. Far across was another mountain range.

FIFTY-FOUR

It was stop-and-go traffic most of the way to Culver City. It was after nine when I pulled up in front of a large apartment complex, following the directions Fat Wally had printed for me in Chicago.

There must have been forty doorbells but none had Susan's name. I checked the mailboxes and found, "S. Keating, L. Payne." But no apartment number was listed.

It was a neighborhood full of similar buildings, all brick and cement and striped-off parking spaces. This was where Susan and Laura had come after they'd "lost the house," and gotten rid of Dan Payne. This was the small apartment Laura had hated. The place with "No pool. No grass or trees or anything."

I checked the parking lot for the car that Dan Payne had bought Susan. Her reward for what?

A shiny blue-gray Lexus was sitting all alone in a back corner. This was one of Susan's old habits, to protect her car from minor parking lot dings.

I parked several spaces away and about twenty minutes later she came hurrying my way. She was dressed for the office but for some reason she didn't look as bright and confident as the woman I'd seen in Chicago.

I got out. "Hi," I said, but she didn't slow down. "Have you heard anything?"

"What are you doing here?" She said without a hint of warmth and opened the door to the Lexus. She was wearing a white jacket over a black blouse and gray dress slacks.

"You told me to come, remember?"

"Sure took you long enough."

"Have you heard anything from Laura?"

She shook her head.

"Can I buy you breakfast? Something I want to show you."

"You know I have a job?"

"You have a daughter, too."

"Okay, okay. There's a Denny's on my way. You want to follow me?"

She closed the door before I could answer. I jogged back to my car and followed along for a mile or so.

Years ago there'd been a Denny's up in Rogers Park. This one didn't look much different. It was a Greek diner without the Greeks.

Susan got right to the point. "Okay. Let's see whatever it is," she said, as the waitress poured coffee. Wrinkles framed her eyes. She'd skipped her makeup session this morning. But that didn't stop me from wanting her.

I slipped the red light photograph out of the folder and across the table.

"How many times am I supposed to look at this?"

"You sure that's not your husband or one of his friends?"

"Who can tell?" she said. "Yeah, it looks a bit like him. But hell, it looks a bit like you too."

"Couple other things," I said, and I slid the credit card log across the table.

"What's this?"

"That pickup is registered to someone named Reginald Reilly," I said. "That's a log of his credit card activity."

"This must have cost," she said, as she skimmed through it.

"It doesn't give us that much," I said. "We already knew that truck was in Chicago. Now we know it wasn't there for long."

"And look at the timing," she said.

"Exactly," I said. "And something else. Your

186

hubby arrested Reilly for burglary about five years ago."

Her head came up. "Dan did?"

I nodded. "But Reilly walked for some reason."

She picked up the red light photograph and gave it a long look. "So this isn't just some guy who happened to run a light. He came to get Laura."

"Sure looks that way."

"I just don't see Dan . . . I mean why would he buy us a house and build Laura a nice new bedroom if he was planning to kidnap her."

"Maybe something happened later."

"What?"

I wasn't giving her Laura's diary. That was mine and mine alone. But I could give her a hint. "Maybe they grabbed some of his money."

"He doesn't have any money!"

"Then how did he buy that big house? How did he buy you and Laura those cars? The trip to Rio. The trip to Florida. Of course, he's got money. Why do you keep lying to me? Where is he?"

She gave me a long look then shook her head. "We've been playing phone tag for two days but somehow we never quite connect. I guess he's ducking me but at least we know he's around. Look, give me some time to find him. Then I'm probably going to need your help."

"I could help you find him," I said.

"That's not a good idea. You should keep far away from him."

"I'm not afraid of Dan Payne."

"Look, if he finds you out here, he'll know we're on to him and then he'll disappear. Is that what you want?"

"We could go to the police."

"That won't work any better than it did in Chicago. Worse. He's got friends here. Look, you just have to trust me, Eddie. Huh? What do you say? Just this once."

This was one of her old complaints: I never trusted her. "So what am I supposed to do all this time?" I said.

"Go fishing. Go to Disneyland," she said. "Drive up the coast. Look, I'll call you tonight and we can get a drink somewhere. Figure out some kind of plan. How's that sound?"

It sounded like nothing but bullshit. But I didn't say that. I said, "Okay."

FIFTY-FIVE

Back in the car, I took a look at my road atlas. I was barely an inch from the Pacific, an ocean I'd never seen. According to the map, Venice Boulevard would lead me straight to the beach. Wasn't this the place with the wide boardwalk, surfers and roller-bladers, and the pot-smoking hippies?

That would be about as much fun as Disneyland, I decided, and dug out Fat Wally's directions to Scott Brasher's address in Van Nuys. It was back near Chatsworth. The freeway crept along except for a steady stream of motorcycles which passed in the narrow space between the lanes.

The house was small and brown. It would have looked right at home in some Midwestern farm town. On either side were homes that would have fit that same small town. One was bright yellow. The other a faded blue. Three frame houses in a row, without a doubt the oldest buildings on the block. The neighbors probably thought of them as eyesores. The new houses were too big, too modern, too much like that soulless house I'd seen in Chatsworth.

For some reason this little dark house brought a smile to my face. I could see Laura here. Maybe it was the basketball hoop above the garage door. Had she and Scott played H-O-R-S-E? Had they sat on this wide front porch, just a single step above the sidewalk, and talked about their future while the rain drummed over their heads?

I climbed that single step but before I got across the porch, I knew the house was empty. There wasn't a curtain on a single window. The sun was shining off bare floors, not a rug or a stick of furniture in sight.

I rang the bell, anyway, and listened to it echo.

Was this the house Laura was talking about in her diary? What was it she'd written? *That's why there's no furniture.* No. That didn't make sense. That was about the Chatsworth house, wasn't it?

Nobody lived in this house.

A car pulled in next door and a woman got out. She was forty or a few years beyond. Her matching blue slacks and jacket looked like a work uniform.

She gave me a big smile. "Hi," she said. "I'm Mary Anne. You moving in?"

I shook my head. "Eddie. I was looking for the Brashers."

The smile faded. "They picked up," she said. "If you'd come by a few days ago you could have

189

helped load a big old U-Haul."

"Do you know where they went?"

"Back to Iowa," she said. "They had a little bad luck here. But it's a good house, Eddie. Don't let that scare you off."

"Not looking for a house," I said. "I'm looking for my daughter Laura. She was a friend of Scott."

She started to smile but then it froze. "You're not Laura's father," she said, and she took a few steps back.

"I'm her real father," I said. RD.

She stopped and the smile came back. "Wait. Wait," she said, and she pointed and snapped her fingers. "You're from Chicago."

"Now how'd you know that?"

"Oh, just something Laura told me one day. Is she okay? I've been worried sick since I heard about Scott."

"I don't know," I said. "That's why I'm here. She came to Chicago but then she disappeared. She's missing."

"Eddie, I don't know what to say," she said, and for a long moment she didn't say anything. "You've come a long way to find an empty house. Would you like a cup of coffee?"

FIFTY-SIX

We sat in the kitchen, at a big round table in the center of the room. Mary Anne got the coffee started and I began talking and I barely stopped. Her eyes were a greenish brown, her hair brown with traces of gray. She sat with her hands circling her coffee cup or folded across her chest. She nodded her head, asked a question now and then, and kept the coffee warm.

I didn't skip much besides Laura's diary and my fun and games with Susan. "This might be the most comfortable kitchen I've ever been in," I said when I couldn't think of anything else to add.

"So where do you go from here?" she asked. "What's the next step?"

"You know, I really don't know what I'm doing. I'm trying to track down her stepfather. I'm looking for that pickup truck. I want to talk to my ex some more. But I don't know. She didn't seem too happy to see me."

"Ex's are like that," she said.

"Got one, too, huh?"

She held up two fingers and flashed a smile. "And I've met yours." Something in her voice told me that they hadn't gotten along.

"She's a tough one," I said.

"She loves Laura and Laura loves her. That's what's important. Dan Payne. Now there's a man I wouldn't trust with . . . Sorry."

"It's okay," I said. "How well do you know him?"

"Not very. But he was around for years, picking Laura up, dropping her off."

"I thought Laura and Scott just got together."

"I think they finally got hot and heavy. But Laura worked and worked on that boy. Scott was a shy one and he was a bit of a mama's boy and then his mother died and he went deeper into his shell. So Laura had to pull him out very, very gently and she did. But she put her time in. Your daughter's a very determined young lady."

"I feel like I hardly know her," I said.

"Eddie, I feel that way about my son and I see him practically every weekend."

"How old?" I asked.

"Twenty-two," she said. "He's at Riverside, studying philosophy of all things. He's a big fan of Nietzsche. If that means anything to you."

"Didn't he play for the Packers?"

She gave me an odd look. "I think you're a little confused."

"I was an engineering major," I said, "And I didn't get far. But I did take an intro to philosophy course. Ray Nitschke was the line backer. Nietzsche was the virgin who died of syphilis. That's probably the only reason I remember him."

"My son says that's only half true."

"Well, he's probably right. But I'll bet I know more about the linebacker. Hey, where did Laura live?" I asked. "They were somewhere around here, right?"

"Come," she said, and gave me a two-finger wave. I followed her through the house and out to the porch. "Right through there." She pointed between two of the big, new houses across the street. "Three, four blocks. I could see it burning from here."

"I thought they lost it in a foreclosure," I said.

"They did. The bank boarded it up, the whole bit. And then a few weeks later it burned to the ground in the middle of the night. I just naturally assumed that was Dan Payne."

"Why?" I asked as we walked back inside.

"I never liked him," she said, "even before he got caught. Ever. He's one of those bullies that give all the good cops a bad name. He likes to undress women with his eyes. And if nobody else is looking, boy does he let you know he's doing it. And I'll bet if you asked him about those women he pulled over and what he did to them, he'd tell you it was all their idea. And he'd believe it, too. And I'm sure he believed it was somehow the banks' fault that he got fired and couldn't make his mortgage payments. So when they took the house over, he probably figured it was his natural born right to burn it down. As if you could really punish a bank."

"So you think he'd kidnap Laura?"

"I wouldn't put it past him," she said. "What are you planning to do when you find him?"

"I haven't figured that out yet," I said.

"You know, I've got a gun around here someplace."

I shook my head. "You're the second person who's tried to give me one."

"I wouldn't mind getting rid of it, to be honest."

"How about Laura's friends? Did you know anybody besides Scott?"

"Iggy lives right around the corner. Should I call him?"

She found a phone book and started paging through it. "This is embarrassing," she said, as she picked up the phone. "I know Iggy's not his real name. But it's the only one I know." She spoke into the phone: "Hi this is Mary Ann, I live around the corner next to the Brashers. No. I know they did. I was wondering if Iggy was home." She held her hand over the phone. "His name is Paul, it turns out."

Ten minutes later he was at the front door. He was well over six feet with long sandy blonde hair but he probably didn't weigh 150 pounds. He wore jeans and sandals, and tinted wire rim eyeglasses.

"Iggy, thanks for coming," Mary Ann said. "This is Eddie Miles, Laura's father."

He reached out to shake hands but I could see confusion in his eyes. "I'm from Chicago," I said, and that did the trick.

"Oh, yes, of course," he said as we shook. "It's nice to meet you, sir."

"Likewise," I said.

"How is Laura?" he said. "Is she okay?"

"I don't know," I admitted. "That's why I'm here. Have you seen her?"

He shook his head.

"How about Scott? When was the last time you saw him?"

His voice dropped. "He gave me his car."

"When was this?"

"A couple of weeks. Just before... "

"Did he say anything?" I asked.

"We talked for a little. But he was in a big hurry."

"Why did he give you his car?" Mary Anne asked.

"He didn't need it," Iggy said. "They were leaving, him and Laura. I guess they must have been taking Laura's car. It's almost brand new."

"Where were they going?"

He shook his head. "He said what I didn't know wouldn't hurt me."

"Did he say anything about Laura's stepfather?"

"He said he was like an evil genius."

194

"What does that mean?"

He shook his head again.

"Anything else?" I asked.

"Just, I don't know. Nothing really. I know he was afraid. He couldn't sit still. And he made me promise to keep the car in the garage until I got new license plates."

"What was he afraid of?"

"Laura's stepfather, I guess."

"What else?"

"Just that he was in a big hurry to go."

"Anything else about her stepfather? Anything about Dan Payne?"

"He said he'd kill him if he got the chance."

"Why?"

He shrugged.

"How about a soda?" Mary Anne said.

"Sure," Iggy said.

I sipped coffee while Mary Anne poured root beer into an ice filled glass.

Iggy stirred the ice with his finger. "Scott said something happened in some house somewhere, something too crazy to believe."

"What house? Where?" I asked.

He shook his head. This was his favorite answer. "He said Laura's stepfather was not that good an electrician, something like that, that's why they caught him."

"Caught him doing what?"

"Or caught on," Iggy said. "I think that was it. Caught on."

"To what?" I said.

He shook his head.

"Did you talk to the police?" Mary Anne asked.

"About what?" Iggy said. "What would I say to them?"

"Any idea what Scott might have been doing in Malibu?" Mary Anne asked.

"That's so weird," Iggy said. "Scott didn't swim."

"Ever?" Mary Anne said.

"He never learned. He said there weren't any oceans in Iowa."

After Iggy left Mary Anne warmed up both our coffees. A few minutes later I said I should be going.

"Where are you staying?"

"Pearblossom or Palmdale," I said. "I'm not sure yet. I feel like all I've been doing since Laura disappeared is wasting time."

FIFTY-SEVEN

The mailman was making his rounds on Revere Street in Chatsworth. There were still no signs of life at 421. I drove around the block. When I got back the mailman was a few doors past Dan Payne's house.

I pulled into the driveway, got out and rang the bell. Nothing. I tried the door. Locked. I checked the mailbox but found nothing but a week's worth of junk mail.

A path led around the side of the house. I followed it. The gate to the back was latched. I reached over, found the clasp, and continued along a path of flagstones to a secluded back yard.

An in-ground swimming pool was bone dry. The grass was overgrown. Thick vegetation grew on all sides, blocking the view of the neighbors. It was a cozy back yard with a small brick patio and plenty of privacy. But there wasn't a stick of furniture. No chairs or chaise lounges. No swing set or sandbox. No barbeque grills. No reason to be out here at all.

Thick, vertical blinds hung on the inside of patio doors. I tried to slide the door but it didn't budge. "Laura," I called. "Laura you in there?" I put my ear to the glass but heard nothing in return. I pulled the door again with the same result.

We'd had patio doors at the house in Avondale and had kept a blocking bar wedged in the track when the door was closed. This was to protect it from burglars. Supposedly this was one of their favorite ways into a house.

I knelt down. The track was clear. I stood up and played around with my pocket knife, twisting it this way and that at various locations between the two doors but the lock held.

I walked out front, popped the trunk, and went looking for Ace's tire iron. A UPS truck drove by and stopped a few houses down. A woman opened the door and took a small package from the driver's hand. The driver jogged back to the truck. But the woman didn't move. She stood there looking my way with the package in hand.

I closed the trunk, got behind the wheel, watched the UPS truck drive away, and still the woman didn't move. The hell with it, I decided. I'd come back after the sun was down.

In Pearblossom, two moving vans were parked in front of the diner. At the motel, the vacancy sign was still lit. I got out and rang the bell but no one answered. The same sign was taped to the door.

I got back in the car. And then I sat there without a destination in mind, wishing I'd asked Iggy a few more questions about Laura.

Was she happy?

A few minutes later the two moving vans pulled out across the way and turned east in front of me. When they cleared, the pickup truck with its distinctive camper top was sitting in front of the diner.

I was frozen in place. I'd found the truck. Now what should I do? After a few minutes of indecision, I called Mike Cantore.

"It's here," I said. "The pickup truck."

"Where?"

"Pearblossom."

"You sure?"

"Absolutely. It's parked outside a diner and it wasn't there two minutes ago."

"Where are you?"

"Down the road by that motel," I said. "You said I could call for advice. You got any suggestions?"

"Don't confront him," he said. "Don't let him see you. Remember he might know what you look like."

"I have to do something."

"Follow him. Wait until he leaves, then see where he goes. He might lead you straight to Laura. But, Jesus, Eddie, be careful. Remember this isn't your line. Maybe you should call my guy out there."

"She could be in the back of that truck."

"I doubt it. She's been gone quite a while. You want to check, wait and do it somewhere where the entire town isn't going to see you."

"There is no town," I said.

"That's even worse," he said and wished me luck. "Let me know what happens."

FIFTY-EIGHT

To hell with it, I decided, and drove straight to the diner. I pulled tight to the far side of the pickup, away from the restaurant's windows and the front door. "Laura," I called softly. "Laura." I reached out and knocked on the camper but there was no sound in return.

The truck looked sturdy. There were dual wheels on the rear axle. The camper top was older than the pickup itself. It was rusted here and there with plenty of nicks and bruises. The windows were thin panels of frosted glass; a slender crack ran through all three. The entire vehicle was coated with sand.

I got out and walked to the rear of the truck. I turned a handle and then lifted the smoked-glass tailgate. There was nothing to see. The back of the truck was empty and spotlessly clean.

A freight truck passed behind me with a roar. As I headed back to the car, a thin guy in denim and a black cowboy hat appeared, coming from the direction of the diner. He looked my way and tipped his hat slightly. I nodded and got back behind the wheel. He got in a dust-covered van and pulled away.

I backed out, then drove back to the motel and parked in an empty slot.

Another pickup pulled in at the diner. Two cars followed.

A few minutes later, two men stepped out of the

diner and stopped in front of the pickup. The taller of the two put one of his cowboy boots up on the truck's bumper. He was an inch or so over six feet, dark and lean with the look of someone who spent most of his days outdoor. I decided he had a rifle or two racked inside the truck. But he didn't look anything like that red light photo.

The other guy I wasn't too sure about. He reminded me of Escrow Jake. He was bald and a bit overweight, maybe five-ten. Like Jake, he looked like he'd never lifted much beyond a racing form.

I watched as they talked and picked their teeth. When they parted, the outdoorsman walked to a sparkling Toyota Camry and headed west. The bald guy got behind the wheel of the pickup truck.

He wasn't in any hurry. He rolled down both windows then adjusted his mirror. As he pulled out, he slipped on a baseball cap. "Oh, yeah," I said and sat up straighter. He could almost be the guy in the red light picture. Almost. I was still a long way from certain.

I gave him a head start, then followed along as he headed east at an easygoing pace. His left turn signal came on after a while and the truck turned left on a cross street.

Before long, the pavement ended. The truck slowed as dust rose into the air. I looked down. The speedometer was perched between five and ten.

We passed a church with a big, empty parking lot then turned right at another unpaved street. It was about as wide as an alley back home. I followed along but suddenly heard Polack Lenny's warning: *"Never go down an alley. You might not come out the other end."*

But it wasn't really an alley. There were houses on both sides laid out on large, fenced-off lots. If the street had been paved, and you added some landscaping to the yards and a bit of size to the houses, it might have looked like Any Suburb, USA.

I kept far enough back that I could just make out the pickup through the dust. Every so often brake lights flashed. The road was rough. I bounced along, now down to about five miles an hour.

There were narrow cross streets every couple hundred feet. I turned left at one, went up a bit then turned right. I could still see the dust of the pickup truck through the wide spaces between the houses.

After a bit, I realized if I rode the edge of the road, I'd avoid the worst of the ruts. I managed to get up to about ten miles an hour. Now I was only slightly behind the pickup. He was due south in his parallel lane.

The power lines stopped. But the fenced in lots went on. Most of the houses were even smaller here. Many of them had firewood stacked outside. Some looked like they'd been built by hand with scavenged lumber. Others were mobile homes, or campers or vans, often up on blocks. Others were camper tops, with or without the pickup trucks.

Soon it was almost nothing but homemade shacks. Even the windows were plywood. This went on block after block after block, one hideout after another. The dust of the pickup truck stayed slightly ahead on my right.

Something shone softly on the left. I slowed for a better look. Two railroads cars, a caboose and an old wooden freight car sparkled in the gloom. They came together to form an L on a large corner lot. Someone had spent a lot of time and energy making them shine. Solid looking stairs led up to a large porch that filled the space between the cars. There was the now familiar stack of firewood, a round table with an umbrella top and several reclining lawn chairs. Plenty of green plants were perched on the railing. It was the best looking place I'd seen in all of Pearblossom.

A horn blared. I laid on the brakes and came to a stop as the pickup crossed right in front of me. The guy behind the wheel was yelling something I couldn't hear. He pulled off his hat and waved it around. He'd almost come to a complete stop, too.

I shrugged, palms out. "Sorry," this was supposed to say. "My fault." I don't know if that message got through but something did. His eyes narrowed. He looked away, looked quickly back, then jumped on the gas and sped off in a cloud of dust.

"Fuck!" I shouted. He wasn't going to lead me to Laura now. I pounded the steering wheel, turned left and went after him.

The pickup turned this way and that. We were speeding now, bouncing along at 20 or 25 miles an hour. Soon even the shacks were gone.

We were in a desert dumping ground--stacks of old tires and construction debris, hollow truck bodies, old furniture, mattresses, dilapidated sofas and easy chairs. Much of it was garbage dumped years, even decades ago, some of it completely unrecognizable, and now it blended into the landscape. I could imagine it going on forever, all the garbage of a city dumped in the middle of nowhere--Earth's garbage dumped on the moon.

The pickup truck zigged and zagged for a while kicking up thick clouds of dust. The truck was too wide to avoid the ruts and I had no problem keeping it and its dust cloud in sight. He was never going to lose me at this rate. But I was lost without him. My only point of reference was the pickup truck. I might have never found my way back to civilization if he hadn't led me right back to Pearblossom Highway.

He picked up a bit of speed as we passed the diner and the road added a lane. He took it easy in the right lane and I followed a few car lengths behind. He couldn't keep driving forever. But where would he stop?

We passed Palmdale and after a while we came to Interstate 5, heavy with traffic but still moving along. I followed him south. Was he taking me back to Chatsworth? No. We turned off on Interstate 210. I had no idea where the road went but I had plenty of gas. We switched over to Route 118 and before long we were right back to Interstate 5, heading north, back the way we'd just come.

A sign warned: PAY ATTENTION OR PAY THE PRICE. I glanced in my rear view mirror and there he was--and this time I had no doubt--the man from the red light camera. He was hunched over the steering wheel of a gray Mercedes Benz, wearing the same baseball cap from the picture in Chicago. One hand was at two o'clock, the other held a cell phone to an ear. He was staring straight at me.

I had to force myself to lower my eyes, to keep driving normally, keeping a steady speed behind the pickup truck, checking the mirror occasionally. After a while, I started memorizing the license number.

Mike Cantore answered on the third ring. "Eddie, can I call you back?"

"No. Look, I found him. We gotta talk."

"Let me get rid of this other call," he said, and he was right back. "You found who?"

"Both of 'em, I think," I said, and I explained what had happened.

"You realize they're probably leading you into some kind of trap," he said. "You gotta get out."

"I know."

"You sure it's the same guy?"

"Absolutely. Same hat and everything."

"Can you read the license number on that Mercedes?" When I recited it he said: "Hold on. Let me get the file." It didn't take long. "That's Dan Payne. I've got the same plate number right in front of me."

"We've got him," I suddenly realized. "We've fucking got him."

"I don't know if I'd go that far," Cantore said. "But now we know for sure that he was the one in Chicago. That's enough to try the police again. The question is: Will they do anything with it?"

"I'm gonna talk to him."

"Eddie, don't!"

"Why not?"

"First of all it's two against one."

"I can lose the pickup," I said. "If I go down an

exit, Payne's got to follow."

"But you're on his home court. And he knows we're on to him. We know he's involved and now he knows it, too. And that means he's dangerous. He kidnapped Laura. Who knows what he did with her."

"So I have nothing to lose."

"Eddie, If he kills you, there's nobody left to look for Laura. Who's going to push the police into action? Nobody. And that means he'll get away with it. Is that what you want?"

"So what should I do?"

"Can you lose him?"

"Sure."

"Remember what I said. Be careful. You die, there's nobody to fight for Laura."

"What about you?"

"Eddie, you already paid my bill."

We were back on the road to Palmdale doing an even 60 when the pickup pulled out to the left lane and overtook a slow moving truck, a freight-hauler pulling double trailers. The pickup truck drifted back to the right lane. I backed off the gas and stayed out in the left lane. Soon Payne and I were both alongside the freight truck. An exit was approaching.

I sped up. At the last possible moment I cut right in front of the truck's bumper. An air horn sounded and brakes hissed. I jumped a slight curb and headed down the exit ramp all alone.

I was at the stop sign at the end of the ramp-- feeling proud of myself--when I looked up and there was the Mercedes coming straight at me. Payne was going the wrong way down the entrance ramp opposite me. He was using the entrance ramp for his own personal exit. He didn't bother stopping at the bottom. If he looked for cross traffic, I didn't notice. He came straight across the road, aiming for a head on crash, swerved at the last possible second and there we were door to door, less than a foot apart, blocking the entire exit ramp.

"Hey, nice driving, hero," he said.

He had a long narrow face with a smile that revealed a full set of very white teeth. He wore a colorful island shirt--something he might have picked up in Rio or Florida. A gold chain sparkled and skin glowed. But the suntan couldn't conceal a couple of tiny warts and several old acne scars. Dark circles surrounded his eyes. His face was drenched with sweat.

He didn't look much like his partner, the man I presumed to be Reginald Reilly. The shape of Payne's face might have been the same, the line of his jaw, the nose, the receding hairline. But there was no softness. No trace of Escrow Jake. No laziness.

He stuck his arm out the window and I ducked. But the arm wasn't for me. He raised it in the air for the car that had come down the ramp behind me. Payne's gesture was full of authority and the car followed it and went around us on the sandy shoulder.

"Where is she?" I said.

"Who's that?"

"Laura. Where is she?"

"Laura? Laura who?"

"Laura your stepdaughter," I said. "Look, I know you took her. I can prove it and I will."

"Okay, tough guy. Stop shaking. Go ahead and prove it."

I reached over, opened my file folder then held up the red light photograph.

"What's that supposed to be?" he said, and his left eye began to twitch.

"That's you running a red light behind me in Chicago."

"Not me," he said and the twitch became more pronounced.

"That's you, all right. Now where is she?"

He pointed at the photo. "You know that kind of looks like a guy I used to know. Looks like his truck, too."

"Yeah," I said. "You guys do look a bit alike. But it's not Reginald Reilly. It's you. Pictures don't lie."

"Are you really that stupid, Miles?" He almost spit the words and just like that the twitch was gone.

"You took her," I said.

"Took her. Took her."

"You kidnapped Laura and you killed Ace."

"Kidnapped? You can't kidnap your own child. Don't you know anything?"

"She's not your child," I said. "She's mine, and I'm taking this straight to the police."

"Take it. Take it. Take it, my friend. But take a look around first. Tell me what you see." He stuck his head out the window and into that narrow space between our cars. Before I could move, he had both hands on my shirt. Buttons popped as he pulled me towards him. My arms were trapped by the narrow

207

window. I tried to find the door latch but couldn't. His arms jerked me upwards towards his own jeering face. "There're holes all over this desert," he said as I hung there helpless. His breath smelled of eucalyptus drops. "I see you out here again, you're going in one." He pushed me away. The Mercedes shot backwards, veered to the right, turned back up the entrance ramp and was gone. The scent of eucalyptus hung in the air.

FIFTY-NINE

I picked up a six pack and a bottle of bourbon and checked in at a Best Western in Palmdale.

What had I been thinking, driving around Pearblossom in a car with Illinois license plates? How smart was that? And worse yet, it was Ace's car, which Payne and Reilly might have seen in Chicago.

Where was Reilly heading on those dusty roads? Would he have led me straight to Laura if I hadn't gotten distracted by those glowing railroad cars? Would I ever see her now?

I had a couple of quick drinks then managed to stop myself. I wasn't getting drunk again. That's how I'd lost Laura the first time. *Think straight*, I told myself.

I had to get into that house in Chatsworth. A crowbar would probably get me through the patio door. I should probably follow the sergeant's advice and get some new clothes. Maybe I could rent a car or, better yet, a pickup truck.

Before I got too far in my planning, the phone rang.

"He says he's gonna kill you next time," Susan said in my ear.

"Who?"

"Dan. Remember him. The guy you're not afraid of. He said you were shaking so bad it was funny."

"Yeah, a laugh riot," I said.

"I can't believe you showed him that picture," she said. "That was our ace in the hole."

"I just wanted him to know."

"Go home, Eddie. Before he finds you again."

"Look, something happened in that house in Chatsworth."

"What?"

"I don't know. But I talked to one of Laura's friends."

"Who?"

"A kid named Iggy."

"I know Iggy."

"He said Scott told him something happened in that house. He wasn't sure what. But he said Scott was terrified of your husband. Whatever it was it sent Laura packing and it probably got Scott killed."

"Or maybe he just drowned."

"Yeah, but Iggy said he didn't know how to swim. So what was he doing in the water."

A minute or more must have passed with just the sound of her breathing. "I'm meeting him in an hour," she said.

"Who?"

"Dan."

"Where?"

"Forget it," she said.

"Chatsworth?"

"No. But that's your last guess."

"Your place."

"He's always been a very good liar," she said. "I want to look into his eyes."

"What am I supposed to do?"

"Just hang tight. I'll call you as soon as I can."

SIXTY

Hang tight. I'd been hanging tight since Laura disappeared. Where had it gotten me?

I poured the remains of the whiskey and beer down a drain, took a cold shower, then got in Ace's car and headed for Chatsworth.

The house on Revere Avenue was dark. The house with the For Sale sign was dark, too. I parked in the driveway, popped the trunk and got out. I found a slender pry bar then walked down the block and across the street.

I followed the flagstone path around the side of the house. The swimming pool was still dry. The grass hadn't been cut.

A soft light glowed beyond the patio doors. I slid the pry bar in between the two doors and moved it up and down underneath the lock. This got me nowhere. So I gave the bar a hard upward jerk and the lock unlatched with a pop. The door slid a few inches. The blinds rattled. I was looking into an empty room. It might have been a family room. This one was for the man without a family. Not a piece of furniture, just a counter at the far end leading into a kitchen.

I stood there for a minute or two, listening, waiting, then slid the door open, parted the blinds and walked in.

The refrigerator kicked in as I passed and that got me jumping. I stopped to catch my breath then moved on, past another room with no furniture towards a dim light in the front of the house. I held the pry bar tight, a club in my right hand.

There was a stairway just inside the front door. Off to the left, light spilled from an open door that led into the garage.

The first two slots were empty. The third slot held a Ford Mustang, with a bench seat sitting on the roof. Was this Laura's car, the one Scott had been arrested in? I peeked inside. The car had been pulled apart, the back seat was out, the floor mats upended, the glove box open.

I left the garage and started slowly up the stairs. One stair creaked. But no sound came from above.

A large, empty room at the top of the stairs was illuminated by street light. I could see marks in the carpet where furniture had once been. I opened a door, flicked a light switch, and looked into a large bathroom with his and her sinks. The next door led into a closet which was about as big as my bedroom. Empty coat hangers hung on parallel bars.

Down the hall, a door had been kicked in. I found a light switch. A long narrow desk had once held various computers. Now it just held parts. The computers had been opened and the insides torn out. Monitors sat with broken screens. Printers had been cracked like egg shells.

I switched the light off, and walked down the hallway to the last door. Even in the dimness of the street lights I could see that the dorm room Dan

Payne had built for Laura had been destroyed.

The mattresses had been torn open and the stuffing pulled out. The dressers, nightstands, and bed frames were in pieces. But someone had gone to the trouble to arrange the ruins into neat piles. A single University of Arizona pennant clung to a wall. Several other pennants were part of the various piles. A broom leaned against a wall. I hit the light switch and a ceiling light came on.

Except for that single pennant, the walls were bare except for a series of uniform holes.

The holes were round, maybe an inch or two from side to side, spaced several feet apart. Something had been covering the holes at one time. You could see glue marks here and there, a small square pattern slightly larger than the circle. Bits of mirrored glass clung to the glue.

Loose wires poked out of several holes. In a corner alcove, two mirrored tiles were still in place. I tried to pry one loose. When that didn't work I used my foot and the mirror shattered.

I started pulling out the shards of the mirror. A circular piece of thick glass was revealed. *High Resolution*, was written around the shiny lens.

"A camera," I said, and I turned one of the shards of glass over and looked right through it--a camera hidden behind a two-way mirror.

"Oh, my god," I said. This was why there was no furniture. Payne didn't want Laura and Scott wasting time in the other rooms or out by the pool.

Cameras that covered every angle. They were the stars of his latest movie.

"Oh, my god." Laura had filled page after page of

her notebook with the same expression. And now I understood. He'd filmed them fucking, a couple of college students having fun in the dorm.

I opened a door which led into a small bathroom. I found the light switch, a toilet, a sink, a shower, and several more holes.

Dan Payne had not wanted to miss anything.

SIXTY-ONE

I kept calling Susan's number but all I got was that same message: *You know the drill.* I left a message. "I found out what happened in Chatsworth. Call me."

I turned off the lights and walked out the front door and down the block to Ace's car. I sat behind the wheel for a while waiting for the phone to ring, then started back for Palmdale.

Back at the hotel, I paced the room. I wanted to punch the walls and suck the whiskey out of the drain. I wanted to stop my brain from turning. I wanted a cigarette, a plate of pasta, a woman in my arms.

It was midnight when the phone finally rang. "He's a fucking liar," Susan said. "I don't know what's true anymore."

"Dan Payne can't tell the truth," I said.

"You met him once and now you're an expert?"

"I found out what happened. That's what he can't tell you."

"What?"

"It's kind of hard…" And I remembered Laura having a hard time telling me in Chicago: *I can't figure out how to say it.* "It'd be easier to just show you," I said. "Can you meet me in Chatsworth?"

"Eddie, I have to work in the morning."

"That's not gonna matter after this."

Susan was waiting in her car when I pulled into the driveway. She got out. "How do we get in?"

"I figured you'd have a key," I said. "But that's okay. I left the front door unlocked."

"What if he's in there?"

I shook my head. "He's not." I'd searched the house from top to bottom before I'd left. Nobody was living here now.

I opened the front door. Susan walked towards the garage.

"Is that Laura's?" I said.

She walked across and poked her head inside the Mustang. "He tore it apart. What was he looking for?"

I shook my head. I didn't know, unless it happened to be his missing money. "Something," I said.

I followed her from the garage to the living room. "What happened to all the furniture?"

"Come on upstairs. I'll show you."

I led her up the stairs and gave her a tour of the second floor. The master bedroom, the destroyed computers, and then down the hallway to the dorm room.

"Oh, my god," she said. "Who did this?"

I watched her closely as she looked at this and that, poking through the piles of garbage with her feet. It didn't take her long to find the mirror I'd broken or the camera hidden behind it.

She looked up and surveyed the room. But she

didn't look my way and she didn't say a word.

It looked like she was about to say something. Her hands went to her mouth. She walked quickly to the bathroom, lifted the seat, and vomited into the toilet. She whirled and punched the medicine cabinet and the mirror splintered and blood ran down her hand. "How could he?" she shouted. "His own...?"

"But she's not, right?"

Susan punched the glass shower door. It didn't break but she left a smear of blood on it and headed out of the room shouting incoherently. I flushed the toilet and grabbed a towel.

Could she be that good an actress?

I followed along behind, wiping up the blood she left in her wake.

I couldn't stop myself from thinking about that film. A section of Laura's diary popped into my head. *"Can you have an orgy with just one other person? Sure can!"*

"The fucker," I shouted. "What was she doing with him, anyway?"

"Oh, Jesus Christ, Eddie, what are you talking about?" Susan shouted back as I followed her out to the hallway.

"Calm down," I said. "Let me see your hand."

She waved the bloody hand in front of me. "Calm down? Calm down?" she shouted. "Tell me how the fuck I'm supposed to do that."

I grabbed her arm and then pulled her towards the light, towards the master bedroom doorway. She'd scraped some of the skin above the knuckles. "It's not too bad," I said, and I wrapped the towel around her hand.

"You're not like him, are you?" Susan said.

"Like who?"

"Like Dan Payne. Tell me you're not."

"I'm not."

"Hold me."

I wrapped her in a hug and we moved around the hallway in tiny steps, a slow, sad, dance. Her body convulsed and tears ran down my neck.

For some reason an image of my high school sweetheart popped into my head. It was the night it ended. *Why was I thinking about her now?*

"I really like you, Eddie. I really do. But nobody's ever going to love you until you love yourself."

"What the fuck does that mean?" I shouted once again to the same old drivel.

"I'm gonna kill him," Susan said. "That's what it means. Will you help me?"

"Of course."

"You promise?"

"I promise."

Before I knew it we were down on the carpet, groping each other like animals in heat; down where the cameras couldn't see us. *Or could they?*

"What are we doing?" Susan shouted before we got too far. "Stop!"

"Sorry," I said.

"Jesus Christ, what's wrong with us?"

I stood, then grabbed Susan's hands and pulled her to her feet. "How could you marry him?" I said.

"Oh, Eddie, don't do this to me. Not now."

We ended up sitting on the top step looking down. Ten minutes must have passed before either one of us spoke.

"I knew something was wrong the day we left," Susan said. "He sent me on a wild goose chase for a lost check. And then as soon as I got to the bank he called to tell me he'd found it. So he came without me to show Laura around. He didn't want me to see what he'd done to this house."

"Maybe we should go to the police," I said.

"No," Susan said.

"Maybe."

"With what? Some holes in a wall."

"We tell them what happened."

"Without Scott and Laura we don't have anything."

"Those cameras."

"Right," she said. "We go to the police, we'll be sitting in a courtroom someday and they'll be playing that video for a jury. You really want that?"

"There is no film," I said. "Laura and Scott destroyed it before they left."

"Do you know one single thing about computers?"

"Those computers are nothing but garbage now."

"The world wide web. You know how that works?"

"Vaguely," I said.

"Do you know what a web cam is?"

That stopped me. "So how do we do it?" I said after a while.

"I need time to think," she said. "And you've got to keep away from him until we're ready. So the first thing we do is switch cars."

"Why?"

"Because I need you, Eddie. And if Dan finds you again you're not going be much help to me."

"He knows your car, too," I said. "Anyway, I want him to find me."

"Not until we're ready," she said.

We turned off the lights, locked up the house, exchanged keys, and then stood in the driveway.

"You know what's funny?" Susan said. "I really wanted this house. Isn't that pathetic? I don't give two shits about Dan Payne. I haven't for years. I wanted this stupid fucking house and look what I did. Look what I did."

"How could you know?" I said. "I mean, who could ever know something like this?"

"And it's just big," she said. "There's nothing special about it. It's just a big, boring house." She walked to Ace's car, opened the door, and got behind the wheel.

"I should come with you," I said. "We should stay together."

"Give me some time to think. Let's talk in the morning. We need a plan. We'll need guns. You sure you're up for this? "

I nodded. "I know where to get a gun," I said.

"Good," she said. "Get it. And I'll call you first thing in the morning and we'll talk about what we're going to do to him."

As I watched her drive away, I realized that Laura's diary was in Ace's glove compartment.

I'd already lost Laura. *I couldn't lose her diary, too.* No. That was mine. It was only paper and ink. But Laura was right there on the page, the good and the bad, the real girl.

SIXTY-TWO

I stayed well back as I followed Ace's car along Devonshire. The Lexus felt like a brand new car. The odometer hadn't yet hit 20,000.

At a red light I fiddled with the controls as Susan got further and further away. But I wasn't worried about losing her. I figured I knew where she was heading. All I really wanted was Laura's diary.

I took the freeway south. Everyone was flying, of course, and I soon found myself flying along with them. The Lexus barely felt like it was moving. By the time I caught myself, I'd almost caught up with Susan. She was one lane over not ten car lengths in front.

I hit the brakes and the car behind me flashed its high beams. I drifted two lanes to my right and kept my foot off the gas pedal. Cars swerved around me and formed a buffer zone between us. And then somewhere around Interstate 10 Susan disappeared. Ace's Toyota was there one minute and gone the next.

I continued south to Venice Boulevard and then headed east. I stopped at a 7-Eleven along the way and poured myself a cup of very dark coffee. I added enough cream to make it drinkable, and then walked up and down the aisles killing time while searching for a snack.

I gave her a half hour or so, then pulled into the parking lot at Susan's building and drove front to back. Ace's car wasn't there. I pulled across the street into another parking lot and found a space where I could see both driveways. I sat there waiting for Ace's car to appear. Before long I was fast asleep.

The phone woke me. "What are you doing?" Susan said.

"Sleeping," I said. "How about you?"

"I'm looking out my window."

"So what's up?"

"You are so stupid," she said. "I'm looking right at you."

"I can explain." I searched the windows across the street for her face but I couldn't find it.

"Don't bother," she said. "You don't trust me. You never have."

"Susan…"

"You gonna stay there all night?"

"Look…"

"Remember that time you followed me in Chicago. You and Laura. Remember how that turned out?"

"Susan, wait!"

"If you don't trust me, why should I trust you?"

"Look, I was worried about you, okay?"

The phone went dead in my ear. I called right back but her phone didn't ring. It went straight to her recorded message.

I pulled out; drove around the block, then back into Susan's parking lot. Ace's car still wasn't there.

I spent an hour or more driving around the neighborhood but I never found Ace's car. Susan had hidden it well.

SIXTY-THREE

In my dreams I heard Susan's voice: *Remember the last time you followed me? Remember how well that turned out?*

I sat up in bed. *Yeah, I remembered.*

I'd already lost the job, was already drinking too much. I wasn't home much. But we were still trying to hold it together, trying to be a family.

It became a regular thing. If I was home at night, Susan would say, "I'm going for a ride." And she'd disappear for an hour, or two or three or four, and leave me to watch Laura. I was convinced she was meeting another man.

One summer night, as soon as she was out the door, I grabbed a sleeping Laura from her bed and hurried down the stairs, blanket and all.

I followed Susan for an hour or more but all she did was drive around the Northwest Side, down one main drag after another, first one way and then the other. She wasn't in any hurry and she didn't seem to have any destination in mind. Maybe she really was just taking a ride, I decided.

Laura woke up and I got distracted and ended up right behind Susan at a red light. "Mom's singing," Laura said. I looked up and there was Susan singing in her rearview mirror. I could hear her radio playing some oldie from long ago.

"Moms!" Laura called.

Susan looked in the mirror then got out of her car and walked back. "What are you doing?"

"Just taking a ride," I said.

She turned around, got back in her car and sped off. I took Laura back home and tucked her in, then waited in the living room.

It was close to dawn when the front door finally opened. "I'm getting a divorce," Susan said. "And I want you out of here." She walked past me and up the stairs and a minute later I heard the shower running.

SIXTY-FOUR

I awoke with the door opening. *Dan Payne,* I thought, and I was out of the bed and charging forward. The maid's head came into view. "Sorry," she said, and quickly disappeared. I looked at the clock. It was a few minutes past noon.

I checked my phone but there wasn't a single message or missed call.

I called Susan over and over and listened to her recorded voice. I called information and they gave me a different phone number for Susan's address in Culver City. But I got the same familiar message. "You know the drill," Susan said just ahead of the beep.

"Would you please call me?" I said. "I can explain about last night." *What would I tell her? Something. Anything.* Anything but the diary. I was hoping that was still safely tucked away in the glove compartment.

After a while I got behind the wheel of Susan's Lexus and headed for Culver City. Ace's car was not to be found. I tried to retrace our route to the Denny's. Susan had said it was on her way to work. But when I did find a Denny's, it wasn't the one we'd stopped at.

I pulled in anyway, dialed Mary Anne's number from the parking lot, and then continued on to that yellow house in Van Nuys.

"Are you okay?" she said when she saw me. She

222

poured me a cup of coffee, left the room briefly then handed me a cardboard shoe box. "It's not loaded. I double checked."

A revolver with a short barrel was wrapped in an oil-stained T-shirt. I turned it this way and that, and checked to make sure it was really unloaded. "SPFLD. MA. S&W USA," was engraved on the side. I put it back in the box, next to a nearly full box of ammunition.

"My ex used to call it a ladies gun," Mary Anne said.

"About my speed."

"Should I really be giving you this?"

I told her about my encounter with Dan Payne and his threat to bury me in the desert. I didn't mention that he'd pulled me out of my own car or anything about the house in Chatsworth.

"So what happens if he finds you again?"

"I guess worst comes to worst, I'm gonna try to shoot him before he shoots me."

"You could call the police."

"Maybe," I said and gestured towards the shoebox. "This is just in case."

A few minutes later, I picked up the shoebox. "I'll bring it back," I said.

"I'd just as soon not see it again," she said. "And remember, you didn't get it here. But come back, anyway. Let me know how it turns out. I'll cook you a celebratory dinner."

She leaned forward and we hugged like old friends. "You smell nice," I said.

"You're a sweet man, Eddie Miles. Please be careful."

SIXTY-FIVE

I drove by the house in Chatsworth, back to Culver City, then to Pearblossom. I pushed SEND over and over on my phone but all I got was that same recording.

I did the entire circuit again. I didn't find Susan or Ace's car. The house in Chatsworth was dark. The pickup truck never appeared.

In the middle of the night, I drove out to Pearblossom and parked alongside that winding side road that Reilly had driven down. I must have dozed off. I woke to a palm hitting the roof of Ace's car. A flashlight beam blinded my eyes.

Dan Payne spoke in my ear: "Didn't I tell you not to come back?"

I couldn't speak. I was trapped in that same seat again unable to move.

The flashlight beam moved down and stopped at my lap. Dan Payne barked a harsh laugh. "Well, goddamn. Ain't that something?"

He turned the flashlight to illuminate one of Laura's childhood dolls. It spoke in a child's voice. "Oh, look at the poor man, couldn't make it to the little boy's room."

I sat up in my Best Western bed, drenched in sweat. I reached out and found the bedside light then dialed Susan's number again.

In the morning I went down to the front desk and got directions to a shopping mall. I found a Sears store, a blue jean jacket, rugged-looking work boots, several snap button shirts, a vest, a variety of baseball caps, and a jack knife in a leather case that I could wear on my belt.

"You got any sun tan in a jar?" I asked.

"Sunless tan lotion." The clerk corrected me and gave me the aisle number. On the way out, I picked up a pair of sunglasses.

I decided to follow the sergeant's advice and concentrate on Reilly. He was a coward. The sergeant had guessed it from his occupations alone. I'd seen it in action when he'd taken off like a scared rabbit at the sight of me.

In Pearblossom, I found the house made of two railroad cars easily enough. I turned and went in the direction Reggie Reilly had been going that day.

I passed shacks and houses on both sides of the road and multiple crossroads which looked like they led to more of the same. I kept straight as the houses got farther apart and eventually came to a fork in the road. I took one branch and then the other as they both rose into the hills. After a while I realized the roads met. It was one big circle with enough hiding places for an army.

There were scattered houses and shacks set back from the road. I found a vantage point up in the hills where I could keep an eye on the fork in the road and also the approach to it. After a while there was a mini rush hour of sorts, people coming home to those shacks and homemade houses. Plenty of cars and pickup trucks passed. But none matched the ones I was hoping to see.

I called Susan over and over and listened to her recorded voice.

"Would you please call me?" I said again and again.

"Should I just keep your car?" I asked Susan's

answering machine. But that didn't get me a reply either.

My skin got darker and darker, and Susan's car got dustier. My new wardrobe relaxed a bit.

I looked up Reilly in the Antelope Valley phone book. No Reginald Reilly but I found five Reilly's listed in Palmdale and two in Pearblossom. I wrote down all the addresses and managed to find every one with the help of a Palmdale map that I borrowed from the Best Western. I sat watching for hours on end, day after day, but I never saw the Reilly I wanted.

I drove up and down those dusty streets. I found another vantage point where I could watch the Y in the road. I was choking on sand dust and boredom. Just about every day I'd take an unpaved road into the mountains and take a few shots at an old wooden fence. So far, the fence was winning.

I drove to Culver City every single day but I never found Susan. The house in Chatsworth was always dark. I tried not to think about what had happened inside.

But at least I had my triangle. Pearblossom to Chatsworth to Culver City. I took it easy on the freeways and tried to keep out of everybody's way. There was always plenty of traffic. During the day, motorcycles passed in the small space between the lanes. At night traffic flew past doing eighty, ninety in the car pool lanes. The lane-marker reflectors lit up the road.

Pearblossom to Chatsworth to Culver City. It was my own personal Bermuda Triangle. Everyone was missing.

SIXTY-SIX

After five days I'd had enough. Maybe Susan and Dan Payne were busy covering their tracks. *Why had I ever trusted her?*

I called Mike Cantore. "I was afraid you were dead," he said. "Any luck?"

"I'm going nuts driving in circles," I said. "Hey, you said you could recommend a detective out here."

"Yeah. Nelson Anderson. He's in North Hollywood. Let me find his number." He was soon back with it. "So tell me what you've been doing."

"Boring myself silly," I said.

"Did you talk to the boyfriend's family?"

"They moved back to Iowa."

"Call 'em."

"I don't know where in Iowa."

"You gotta do it, Eddie. You don't check out one lead, that's the one that would have led you right in. Remember that red-light photograph."

"Yeah. You were right about that," I said.

"Hey, when you talk to Anderson, don't tell him how much I charged you. He'll think I'm on the skids for sure."

I hung up then called Nelson Anderson's number and made an appointment for the next afternoon.

I took another trip out to Pearblossom and found nothing but sand.

On the way to the Best Western, I took a detour down Oakdale Street which ended in a cul-de-sac. One of the Reilly's I'd found in the phone book lived towards the end of the block. It was a one-story house covered with faded siding, and would have looked right at home next to those three small houses in Van Nuys.

I'd staked this house out for a few hours on several different days and had driven by at other times looking for Reginald Reilly or his pickup truck. But all I'd seen was the same blue car that was parked there now.

As I was passing, a young woman stepped out of the car. She was fit and sexy looking, sporting short black hair, jeans, and a stylish black leather jacket, a sister to the one I'd bought Laura.

I pulled into the driveway next door, preparing to make a U-turn. The girl reached back into the car and came out with a couple of plastic grocery bags. She turned my way to close the door with the side of her leg. That wasn't a sister at all, I realized, and suddenly found myself shivering in the desert.

The bulldog zipper pull glittered in the afternoon sun. That was Laura's jacket.

SIXTY-SEVEN

There was a strip mall out on the boulevard with a Laundromat on the back corner. I parked in the very last space looking towards Oakdale Street and the Reilly house. I could see the front of the house and the blue car parked in the driveway.

I got out, walked into the Laundromat, bought a Coke from a vending machine and stood in front sipping it. From here I could see the front door of the house but not the car. I tossed the half full Coke in the trash, went back to the Lexus, opened and closed the trunk, then got back behind the wheel.

The sun went down and I stayed where I was. What I was waiting for? I bought a bag of chips and then another Coke. And then the girl came out, got in the blue car and pulled away. She drove right past me, wearing that snazzy black leather. I could hear the radio playing. She was singing along with the song.

Mary Anne's gun fit nicely in the inside pocket of my blue jean jacket. I left the car and walked down the block and across the street. The front door was locked. On the way around the side of the house, I stopped by the attached garage, bent down and pulled. The door started to rise.

I raised it just enough to duck under. I came up right next to a pickup truck. But it didn't look like the one I'd been searching for. I was in semi-darkness in the narrow aisle alongside the truck, a battered wreck that looked like it had survived multiple accidents. The side of the truck had scrape marks front to back. The rear tire was flat, the front fender crushed.

The rest of the garage was thick with cartons and miscellaneous furniture stacked floor to ceiling in a haphazard fashion. *Was this the furniture that had been in that house in Chatsworth?*

Light spilled from a doorway just ahead of me. I moved towards it then a man's voice stopped me. "You forget something, honey?"

I pulled the gun from my pocket and waited out the silence. "That you out there, Dan?" the same voice called before too long. "You come to finish me off?"

I moved slowly forward, towards that lighted doorway, towards that voice.

"Well, come on, Dan. Get in here and get it over with. I'm sick of waiting on you, Payne. I've been waiting on you too many years. Look what it got me. Just look what I got. I would have been better off in prison. Payne? Payne? Payne?"

I came around the corner. Straight ahead was a darkened kitchen. I went left and there he was, hunkered down in a reclining chair with a cane held like a shield in his hand, Reginald Reilly, with his body covered in multiple bandages and casts. Both eyes were blackened. His skull was covered with white tape. His jaw was blue and yellow. He had a large blue cast on one leg and smaller white ones on both arms. A piss line ran down to a bucket next to the chair. If he'd ever looked anything like Dan Payne that resemblance was gone. He now looked like an advertisement for a personal injury attorney.

"Who the hell are you, Mister?" He shouted. "And what the hell are you doing in my house?"

"Where is she?"

"Who are you? Whyon't you tell me that?"

"Where is she?" I said again.

"You can't shoot me without you telling me who you are."

"Where's Laura?" I said as I moved closer.

"Eddie Miles," he said. "My lucky fucking day. I told him you'd be back."

"Where is she?"

He threw his cane away. It bounced off the sofa and a coffee table then rattled around on the floor.

He tried to hold up both hands. But he couldn't get them very high. "You can kill me all you want. Maybe I deserve it. But with god as my witness, I had nothing to do with what happened to your girl."

I sat on the sofa. "What happened?"

"She...She...She...She's...She's..."

He might have gone on like that forever. I got up. "I know she's dead," I said. I slapped him, first with an open hand then with the gun. *She's dead!* My own voice echoed in my head and I realized I'd known this for a while. "Tell me what happened," I said.

"She choked."

I slapped him again, harder. "Tell me how she died!"

"Swear to god, Mr. Miles. She choked on a hamburger. I think she did it on purpose."

"You think she choked herself?" I slapped him again and again and again. Reilly screamed as I kept slapping and then we both ran out of steam.

"God's honest truth," he said after he caught his breath. "He was gonna kill her one way or the other. I didn't realize it at the time but she did. She was a stubborn little girl, your daughter. She wouldn't tell him anything. He'd be riding in back with her and then he'd pound on the wall for me to stop so he could get up front and I swear to god he'd be so mad sometimes his face would be beet red and he couldn't talk for miles. He'd just be kicking that poor old floor. Like to kick a hole in it."

"Tell me how it happened," I said.

"Mister, I was driving. I wasn't back there 'cept once. I didn't know for a thousand miles and that's the truth."

"Tell me," I said. "From the beginning."

It took him an hour or more, with stops and starts and several cigarette breaks.

Payne had called and told him he needed him for a couple of days. In Chicago, they went straight to Ace's. But Reilly had no idea how Payne had found the place. Before too long, I pulled up in my cab and went inside and came out with Laura. They followed us all over town that night.

After I dropped Laura, they waited until the lights went off. Then they walked around the house and Reggie picked the lock on the French doors. "Something I picked up in finishing school," he said.

Laura came out of the bathroom with a toothbrush in her hand. "She screamed so loud I thought she'd wake the whole damn city. Payne hit her and her legs went out from under her and she was down and out."

Ace showed up in pajamas and quickly turned around. Payne went after him and when he came back he was in a big hurry to leave.

Payne bound Laura hand and foot while Reggie packed her stuff in garbage bags from the kitchen. "He was looking for something," Reilly said. "But I never figured out what."

"Money?"

"No. Money was in her backpack. He found that right off."

They rolled Laura in a rug from the basement and carried her out to the truck. They took turns driving. Reilly tried to sleep in the back once but he couldn't do it. Laura was still tied hands and feet. She was on her side tied to the wall of the camper with the gag in her mouth.

"She couldn't really talk," Reilly said. "But she could whisper and what she kept whispering over and over was for me to untie her. She begged and begged. She told me he was gonna kill her. I swear to god if I believed her I might have untied her even knowing Payne would have killed me for sure. You gotta believe me, Mr. Miles. I got a daughter myself. He would have killed me and she wouldn't have got away no how. After that I'd just doze in the front seat. I didn't want to look in those eyes again."

"When did she die?"

"If I was to take a guess, I would say somewhere around the Colorado line. That's where Payne got all funny and then we suddenly changed directions."

"What happened?"

"We stopped for gas and everything changed. He's pacing up and down, then he's on the phone for a while, and when he gets back in the truck we're going to Wyoming instead. Don't ask me why. I never figured that one out."

"What did you do in Wyoming?"

"We went to some town a million miles off the highway. Stayed in a motel. That's when I started to suspect that something was wrong 'cause he never brought her inside. She would have frozen to death in the back of that truck. Next day, we were in Utah and they had some test section where you could drive eighty miles an hour. I got her up there a bit. Payne was sleeping but he suddenly comes awake and he's yelling at me to slow down. And that's when he told me. Said, 'You wanna get pulled over with a body in back?' That's when I knew for sure."

"So what's this choking story?"

"That's what he told me. She choked on a hamburger. He said he fed her and gagged her. When he went back next time she was dead. See I figure she must have hid that hamburger in her mouth and waited until he left."

"Pretty hard to choke yourself, you ask me," I said. "So what did he do with her? Where is she?"

"Somewhere out back door way."

"Where?"

"Sorry. Somewhere off Pearblossom Highway. Somewhere out in that desert. Only way you'll find her is if he shows you. But why would he do that?"

"How'd you guys hook up, anyway?"

"He arrested me, believe it or not. Don't that beat all?"

"I believe you all right," I said. "And then he got on the witness stand and lied to get you out of it. Now why would he do that?"

That stopped him for a few seconds. "You got a little more than I thought you had, Mr. Miles."

"So why?"

"Once he saw my record that's when he got interested."

"Pimping?"

"Hell, I never pimped nobody in my life. What I did, I did some talent scouting for the movies years and years ago."

"What kind of movies?"

"I got the feeling you already know the answer to that one, too," he said. "Kind full of tits and ass."

"What's that got to do with Payne?"

"The man fancies himself a porn star. He's got this big ol' cock he likes to show off. But old Dan can't act worth a damn. Can't fuck very good either, at least not for the screen. So then he decided he was gonna be a producer. Yeah. I tried to help him out but he don't listen all that well."

"You help him set up that house in Chatsworth?"

"What house? I don't know any house in Chatsworth."

"Where were you going that day in Pearblossom?"

"What day was that?"

"The day I almost ran into you."

"Goin' to meet Payne at his lodge. It's just a shack up in the hills. No electricity. No plumbing. Some old prospecting shack with one window. Yeah. He was pissed I didn't bring you there."

"How do I find it?"

"Ain't that easy."

"Just tell me how to find it," I said.

He gave me detailed directions. There were no street signs, of course. It was all landmarks, Joshua trees, and rocks with strange shapes. "There's a crossroad and right after another road angles off to the right. Don't take it. Look to your left and you'll see another road looks like it's heading down. That's the one you want. Follow that around and it'll start to go up. Now I was you, that's where I'd get out and start walking. He'll probably still hear you coming. But he's for sure gonna hear if you drive."

I wrote it all down on the back of some junk mail. "So why won't he be there?"

"Oh, he might stop by now and then if he needs something. He keeps all his old prospecting tools there and special desert clothes. Keeps extra gas for his ATV. But he don't sleep there. Nothing like that. He's a man's man, likes sleeping under the stars."

I put the gun away and pulled out my jack knife. "Tell me where he is or I'm gonna start cutting."

"Mister, I wish I knew where he was. That desert is twenty-five thousand square miles. And he's probably hiding out in one of 'em. But you're never gonna find him. And that's good because you ain't a killer and he is. And you can put that knife away. You ain't never gonna use it."

I followed his advice and put the knife away. I pulled out the gun instead.

"This might be easier," I said. I put the barrel against his leg cast. At the last second I turned it away and fired into the chair.

That got me a bit of respect. He sat up straighter and we both listened to the gunshot echo.

"Where is he?" I said, and for the first time I felt I could actually shoot another human---as long as that human happened to be Dan Payne.

"You can shoot me and my damn chair all you want. I don't know where he is. And I ain't never gonna know cause I really do not know. I'll tell you what. Why don't you call the police? They're already looking for him. I'll tell them everything I know. All they got to do is give me immunity."

"Why are they looking for him?"

"Some kid in Santa Monica. They say Payne

bonded him out of jail and by the next morning he was dead in the water."

"That's interesting," I said. Was *now the time to call the police?* "So who was this kid?"

He shook his head. "Mister, I don't want you getting the wrong idea about me and Dan Payne. We're not friends. We never were. He doesn't tell me his secrets and I don't tell him mine. He helped me out of a jam one day. Kept me out of jail and ever since I've been doing him little favors to pay him back and that's really it."

"Little favors? You let him kill Laura in the back of your truck and you're not friends? You bought all the gas for four thousand miles and you're not friends? You really think I'm that stupid?."

He held up his hands as far as they would go. "Now you're getting things mixed up," he said. "Number one, that's Payne's truck not mine. Mine is sitting right out in that garage. Number two, I didn't pay for nothing but cigarettes and coffee the whole damn trip."

"You know, I was almost beginning to believe you," I said. "That truck's registered to you and you used your credit card for gas and motels the entire trip. And I can prove it."

"Credit card? Who in their right mind would give me a credit card? The last time I worked on the books was 1989."

I remembered that the pickup truck was registered at a phony address in Bay City, the town that Payne had once patrolled. And suddenly I believed Reilly. I realized why Payne might have helped him out of that jam. "He was setting you up to take the fall," I said. "You know you guys look enough alike to be brothers."

"Oh, don't tell me that."

"What am I gonna do with you?" I said. "I can't just leave you here."

"Why not? I can't hurt you. Take my crutches. What am I gonna do?"

"Where's your phone?"

"In the kitchen," he said.

"Your cell phone," I said.

"Lost it."

I pointed the gun at his leg again. He reached into his robe and brought out the cell phone.

"When's your girl coming back?"

"What do you know about her?"

"I know she's walking around in Laura's jacket."

"Mister, I really don't care what you do to me, but please leave my girl out of it."

"You tell her you took that jacket off a dead girl?"

"Look, I ain't never been much of a father," he said. "I'm sorry about your girl. I just wanted to give mine something nice for a change."

"Me too," I whispered on my way to the garage.

I came back with a length of rope. I looped it around his waist a couple of times and then tied it behind the chair. "Your daughter can let you go when she gets back."

"She's not coming until Friday."

I realized I had no idea what day it was. "She'll come tomorrow when you don't answer the phone," I said.

I took a quick tour of the house. I looked under the beds and in the closets but no one was hiding. I crawled up a pull-down ladder but found nothing but joists. "Where's the door to the basement?" I called.

That brought a laugh. "Ain't no basements out here."

I went out to the kitchen, cut the wire on a wall phone, and gathered up all the crackers, cookies, and bottled water I could find. I put it all on the table alongside Reilly's chair. "That should keep you," I said, and I handed him the TV remote.

"This has been some week. First I get beat near to death and end up in the hospital then I get tied up in my own damn chair."

"Who beat you, anyway?"

"Dan Payne. Who else?"

"Why?"

"Why? Who the hell knows with Payne? He said I ran some red light somewhere. But I'll be damned if I remember."

"It wasn't you," I said. "It was Payne. I've got the picture out in the car."

"Well, if you ever find the son of a bitch, you be sure to show it to him. Maybe he'll come on out and un-beat me. What do you think about that?"

SIXTY-EIGHT

I went back to my motel room but I couldn't sit still. I paced for about thirty seconds, then I called Susan and waited for the beep.

"Look, you gotta call me," I said. "I found out what happened to Laura. It's not good news. But I gotta talk to you. I don't know what to do. Please call me back. Please."

I waited for a call that never came then got back in Susan's Lexus and headed to Pearblossom. I tried to follow Reilly's directions into the hills. This was the same general direction where I'd been going to take target practice. But that was in daylight. At night all the landmarks Reilly had given me were lost in the darkness.

I went back to my triangle instead. From Pearblossom to Chatsworth . . . And that's where it ended, with Ace's Toyota parked in Dan Payne's driveway and lights burning behind a second floor window.

The house with the For Sale sign was dark. I backed Susan's Lexus into the driveway and found a crowbar in the trunk. I walked down the block and across the street, with the revolver a soothing weight in a jacket pocket.

I tried the front door then followed the flagstone path around the side of the house. I used the pry bar to pop the patio doors open and then waited until the sound died to slip inside. The only sound was the hum of the refrigerator. I stopped to catch my breath and slip the gun out of my jacket, and then moved on.

The door to the garage stood open. I flicked the light switch. The first two slots were still empty. The seat was still sitting on top of Laura's Mustang. But something had changed. A small pool of oil lay on the floor in the center bay. Red oil. Transmission fluid.

I turned and started for the stairs. Before I got there I slipped. There was more fluid on the hallway floor. But it wasn't transmission fluid at all, I realized. It was blood. I went back to the garage for a closer look. That was blood, too. A pool of blood with a clump of blond hair floating on top. *Susan!*

I found a roll of paper towels on a workbench and wiped the blood from my boots. I skirted the blood on the hallway floor and crept slowly up the stairs. Halfway up, my hand hit the first of two bungee cords that lay like tripwires across the stairway.

Upstairs almost nothing had changed. I moved from room to room and found no one, nothing but some broken computers.

Light spilled from the dorm room--the pornographer's stage. Everything was still in place. Almost everything. A camera had been placed on top of the nearest pile of garbage. It was staring straight at me.

I retreated and stood at the top of the stairs. Laura was dead. That was certain. *Was Susan dead, too?*

The gun was still in my hand but there was no one to shoot. I slipped it into my jacket pocket. I sat on the top step for a minute or two, then went halfway down and stopped at those bungee cords. What was their meaning? More minutes passed and I had no answer. The only answer was that blood with that clump of Susan's hair floating like pond scum.

I was still pondering when I heard the garage door begin to rise. I pulled the gun from my pocket and went up a few stairs. I found myself afraid to move. Should I go up or down? I needed a place to hide. Somewhere I could wait in ambush. Could I shoot him from up here?

I heard a car glide into the garage. The engine died. The door went back down. And then nothing.

I stood on the stairs and waited with the gun pointing towards that lighted doorway. I realized I'd forgotten to switch off the garage lights. Was Payne sitting there watching the door, waiting for me to make the first move?

I found myself silently chanting, "I'm not afraid to die. I'm not afraid to die." I must have told myself this fifty times before I said fuck it. If he wouldn't come out of the car, I'd shoot him right where he sat. But I still couldn't make myself move. I began a new chant. "Susan. Susan." And then I tried another. "Laura. Laura. Laura." And that did the trick. I came down the stairs slowly the chant still going on and on in my head.

I raised the gun in a two-handed grip and then moved towards the garage. I could see the back of Payne's car sitting in the middle spot. As I walked in, the door of the Mercedes began to open. *Too late to turn back.* I hurried forward and fired without really aiming. A leg was half out. I slammed into the door and heard a very satisfying answering cry then aimed through the glass at the contorted face behind it.

"Eddie!" Susan shouted.

I turned the gun away as it fired. "Jesus Christ," I said, and bounced off a nearby work bench, scattering tools as I went.

"Fuck," Susan said. She pushed the door wide but stayed in the seat. "What are you doing?" She stopped to catch her breath. "Are you nuts?"

"I thought you were him," I said. I could barely talk. My heart was pounding. The gun was still there in my shaking hand. My whole body was shaking. I let the arm fall to my side. "I thought you were him. I thought you were Dan Payne."

"Oh, Christ, Eddie." She stood. "Can't you do anything right?" Her face was spotted. Her clothes were soiled. Blood. She was stained head to toe with blood. Her shoes and pants were caked with sand.

"Where is he?" I said. "What happened?"

She moved away from the car. Her clothes were a mess. Her blouse was torn. "He wanted to disappear," she said. "So I did it for him. You're just in time to help me clean up."

"Why didn't you call me?" I said.

"Why didn't you just follow me again?"

"I could have helped."

"Eddie, you didn't let this happen. I did."

"You know about Laura?"

"I know he killed her."

"How?" I said. "Where? What did he say?"

"He said it was an accident."

"When?"

"Eddie, I'm sorry. I didn't get all the details. And put that gun away, would you?" I slipped the gun into my jacket. "He said she was sleeping in the back of that pickup truck and there was an exhaust leak."

"That's bullshit."

"I know."

"Why didn't you let me help?"

"You did, Eddie. Believe me. You were the bait, you and your car. I told him you were here, that you found something you wanted me to see. And he came running to get you. I told him that you were talking crazy, that I was afraid of you, that I still hated you."

"Where is she? What did he do with her?"

"He said he buried her near Pearblossom."

"Where?"

"He wanted to show me. But I wasn't driving around the desert with him. He knew it too well. And I didn't think it really mattered. I figured he was ready for his own grave."

I could see she was proud of herself. Mighty Mom rides to the rescue. Of course, she was a bit late. But who was I to complain? I was even later.

"How could you marry him?"

"Oh, come on."

"No. Really. How could you?"

"He was fine until he got fired and then he snapped," she said. "Sound familiar?" She rubbed her leg where I'd hit it with the car door. "Damn, that hurts."

"Did you give him a blow job when he pulled you over?"

"Eddie. Lay off. I gave him plenty of blow jobs but that doesn't have anything to do with what happened. Grab one of those garbage bags, would you?"

I pulled a heavy-duty garbage bag from a box on the work bench.

"I'm going to take a shower," she said. She handed me the key to Ace's car. "Grab my overnight bag from the trunk, would you?"

When I got back, I found her stripped down to panties. "How do these look?" she asked. "Is there any blood?" She turned around.

"The back," I said, and she slipped them off. She had several bruises and plenty of blood stains but it appeared that none of the blood was her own.

She dropped the panties into the garbage bag with the rest of her bloody clothes then handed me the bag. "Throw that in a garbage can somewhere, and then go get us some food. One of the drive-thru's ought to be open. I'm starving. Get a bunch. And coffee. A couple of large coffees for me, lots of cream and sugar. And then get back here and help me clean this place up."

She tiptoed around the blood on the hallway floor, then stopped on her way up the stairs and turned to give me a better view. "We deserve to go to hell for letting this happen," she said.

She reached down to unhook the bungee cords and then tossed them to the foot of the stairs. They landed in that circle of blood. "You should have seen him fly," she said.

SIXTY-NINE

I carried the garbage bag out the front door, got behind the wheel of Ace's car, and then drove out to Devonshire and pulled into a drive-thru. I ordered hamburgers, fries, coffee and Cokes. While waiting in line, I leaned over and opened the glove box. Laura's diary was right where I'd left it. I set it on the seat beside me.

I picked up the food and started back then missed my turn. I kept right on, past the street that led to Revere Avenue. I went out to the interstate, up to

Palmdale and out to Pearblossom Road where there was nobody but me.

The Vacancy sign was burning at the Starlight Motel but the rest of Pearblossom was dark. My phone rang but I ignored it. I kept on, out to Interstate 15 and turned north. Before long, the bright lights of Las Vegas were shining away in the middle of the night, and then it was dawn and I was cutting through Arizona, passing those strange canyon walls.

I stopped in Utah for gas and more coffee. A hundred miles later a sign read "I-70 Denver," and an arrow pointed the way. I followed it through the mountains. Most of the traffic was long haul trucks. I pulled in between a couple and rode along until a steep grade slowed them down.

Denver was long hours away. It was night again by the time I went through. I followed signs for Omaha, and ended up on Interstate 76.

I wasn't far out of Denver when the snow began to fall. By the time I hit the Nebraska line and Interstate 80 the highway was completely snow covered.

The snow didn't seem to bother the big trucks. Not at first. They kept passing out in the left lane, throwing snow in a blinding fury as I gripped the steering wheel and tried to keep the small Toyota somewhat straight.

Before long the wind picked up and even the big trucks were having problems. I passed several in the ditch and watched another slide across the highway.

We were almost to Ogallala when lights flashed through the snow.

I-80 CLOSED WHEN FLASHING
PREPARE TO EXIT

The highway came to a stop before the exit and then we crawled through the blowing snow for a while. The windshield wipers were barely keeping up.

Ogallala. I'd stopped here on the way west. This had been one of the pickup truck's gas stops. The pump jockey had remembered the driver spending a long time at the pay phone. And I'd found a couple of fresh phone numbers scrawled on the counter.

I-80 CLOSED WHEN FLASHING.
EXIT HERE.

Crossing gates blocked the highway.

At the bottom of the ramp I could barely read a sign that said FOOD AND LODGING. Arrows pointed in both directions. I turned right and soon found myself standing in line at the front desk of a Comfort Inn brushing off the snow.

"You're one lucky fellow," the desk clerk said when my turn came.

"Why's that?"

"They just closed the highway."

"What's so lucky about that?"

"You're getting the last room." He handed me a

key card. "Say your prayers. A couple years back it was closed for six days."

"That'd be alright with me," I said, and got back in my car and slid around to a parking space.

I opened the trunk and that's when I realized that my suitcase was still at the Best Western in Palmdale, a thousand miles away.

I checked the back seat. There were coffee and soft drink cups, plenty of fast food wrappers, and the garbage bag with Susan's clothes.

I tucked Laura's diary into a jacket pocket then carried the garbage bag through the snow. I went up the stairs and down the hall to my room. I brushed snow off, kicked off my boots, then parted the curtains and looked out at the swirling whiteness.

Where was I running to? It was only now that I'd finally stopped that the question hit me. Home, of course. I was already halfway there. But what awaited me in Chicago? Nothing except streets full of bad memories and a future of driving in circles. *What would I tell my friends when they asked about Laura?*

I looked down. Ace's car had already disappeared. It was barely a lump in a sea of whiteness. *What could I say?*

I'd never seen the ocean, I realized in the middle of a blizzard.

I'd never seen the bodies, either. I knew in my heart that Laura was dead. But what about Dan Payne? Was that really his blood?

I began pulling Susan's clothes from the garbage bag and laying it out on the bed. Her denim shirt was first. It was a nicely faded blue, with dark blue striping on the sides and blood stains on both sleeves. The rest of her clothes followed. The sexy bra went on top of the shirt. The tiny panties on top of the blue jeans which were heavy with blood.

The shoes and socks had been soaked through with blood and sand. By the time I laid them on the bed my hands were gritty with it. There was no question it was blood.

But was it Dan Payne's?

To believe anything else would mean that Susan was a monster, too; that she knew all about the trap Dan Payne had laid for Laura; that she'd been part of it from the very beginning.

And then for the finale she'd dreamed up this bloody fashion show. She'd bought the blood at the local butcher shop and then she and Dan Payne had had a good time laughing together while artfully applying it.

No. I would never believe that, any more than Laura had.

I trusted Susan, for a moment or two.

As I started to undress, my pocket notebook fell to the floor.

I picked it up and opened it to the page with the two numbers I'd copied from the phone booth across the way, numbers that were unquestionably written by Dan Payne. One of the numbers was circled. It belonged to the Leadership School in Wyoming.

Why had Payne called the school? Was he setting up an alibi or just trying to add to the confusion? I'd never know the answer but one thing was certain. He wasn't planning to enroll Laura. She was already dead.

The other phone number, I realized for the first time, was to Susan's land line in Culver City.

That stopped me.

After a while, I pulled out my phone and punched in the number. *What would I say if she answered?*

I didn't know anything more than I'd known before, I realized as my phone searched for a connection. Maybe Payne had never actually dialed the number. Maybe Susan had never answered the call.

I pushed the button to end the call. Susan's degree of guilt didn't mean a thing to me. Neither did Susan. Not anymore.

Laura was dead. I could have saved her but I didn't.

Nothing else mattered. All the rest was just a diversion to take my mind off that horrible truth. I'd had a chance to save her but I'd played tour guide instead.

I moved Susan's clothes to the side and crawled under the covers. The gods had closed that highway, I realized, as the snow beat against the building and the wind howled. They'd trapped me in a snowstorm in the middle of nowhere. Except it really wasn't nowhere, was it? Somewhere out here Laura had died, alone and helpless, a prisoner in the back of a westbound pickup truck.

I vowed then that I would never throw Susan's clothes away or Laura's pink book. I would keep them handy until the day I died. And anytime I got carried away with myself--if I ever started believing I was anything like a real man--I would pull them out, souvenirs that weren't rightfully mine, and I would say. "That's what you let happen to your only child. That's who you are."

It was another one for the rule book. A simple one this time. Always protect your blood. I'd learned the lesson the hard way but much too late.

The only blood I had was gone.

Books by Jack Clark

Eddie Miles novels
Back Door to L.A.
Nobody's Angel

Nick Acropolis novels
Dancing on Graves
Highway Side
Westerfield's Chain

With Mary Jo Clark
On the Home Front
Mary Jo Clark as told to Jack Clark
Private Path: The Desk Calendars of
Mary Jo Ryan 1937 – 1943.
Edited by Jack Clark

Stories
Hack Writing & Other Stories

Coming soon:
Criminal Justice & Other Stories
We Haul Anything Cartage Co.

Someday maybe:
The B Side of Misty
Eddie Miles in Paris

ACKNOWLEDGMENTS

I couldn't have done it alone. I'd like to thank Charles Ardai, Pat Arden, Scott Baker, Michele Barale, Vince Clark, Caitlin Devitt, Marilyn Fisker, Steve Grossman, Francis Leroux, Sydney Lewis, Mike Ramsey, and Mary Valentin.

Made in the USA
Las Vegas, NV
21 November 2024